A Dream of Horses
& other stories

A Dream of Horses
& other stories

AASHISH KAUL

Introduction by Scott Esposito

Winchester, UK
Washington, USA

First published by Roundfire Books, 2014
Roundfire Books is an imprint of John Hunt Publishing Ltd., Laurel House, Station Approach,
Alresford, Hants, SO24 9JH, UK
office1@jhpbooks.net
www.johnhuntpublishing.com
www.roundfire-books.com

For distributor details and how to order please visit the 'Ordering' section on our website.

Text copyright: Aashish Kaul 2013
Introduction copyright: Scott Esposito 2013

ISBN: 978 1 78279 536 0

A CIP catalogue record for this book is available from the British Library.

Design: Stuart Davies

Printed in the USA by Edwards Brothers Malloy

We operate a distinctive and ethical publishing philosophy in all
areas of our business, from our global network of authors to
production and worldwide distribution.

CONTENTS

Aashish Kaul was born in New Delhi and now lives in Sydney. He read law in India, and is currently completing a doctorate in arts at the University of Sydney. His work has previously appeared in publications in Australia and the United States.

Scott Esposito is the co-author of *The End of Oulipo?* (Zero Books, 2013). His work has appeared in the *Times Literary Supplement*, *The White Review*, *Bookforum*, *The Washington Post*, *The Believer*, *Tin House*, *The American Reader*, *Music & Literature*, and numerous others. He edits *The Quarterly Conversation* and is a Senior Editor with TWO LINES.

Introduction

Buried deep within *A Dream of Horses* we find a library alongside a church, both perched out over an abyss. It is just the thing, one realizes suddenly, exactly the thing we should expect to see tucked among these seven dreams that Aashish Kaul has persuaded us to take for reality: literature has always impinged on spirituality's turf, and in this book we are in the presence of an intelligence that can make from this overlap truth's hard diamonds. The caretaker of this library knows his books so well that he can tell them by the sound of their pages as they turn. I picture him as a hunched, solid man who will spend a day in the medieval work of turning out a page of fair copy in some ancient script, as indifferent to the changing of the seasons as a mammoth granite. His library on the edge of a void is not, like Borges's Library of Babel, infinite; quite the opposite, it is all too finite, not having acquired a new piece in a decade. Yet within this modest chunk of the eternal, Kaul is capable of uttering that which is unceasing about literature: "Countless unread stories awaited me to set them free of the very words that held them captive. If only I would read them and allow them refuge in my head where, free of a form or structure, they could float at leisure. I was tempted to liberate them, to read them, one after the other, till I had set the very last one free. How ephemeral, I thought, is the process of creation, of writing books, of lending random words to equally random thoughts merely to grant another the privilege of release." This task, it seems, humanity will never tire of. How blessed to make the acquaintance of one of our kind who does it with such immense faculty.

Can it possibly be a coincidence that the seven protagonists of these seven tales are all lone individuals, half-wandering, half-questing through the abyss? That balm of release that the man finds in the library is what they all seek, consciously or not. They are drawn toward it, powered by it, done and undone through it.

I believe it is meaningful that the library hangs out over emptiness, because Kaul clearly belongs to that band of writers whom one of their number has termed "explorers of the abyss." These are people who take it for granted that reality is obscure, befogged, and impenetrable, and they do not write literature toward the real so much as against our foolish, too-widespread assumption that we can easily know it. They began, perhaps, with the likes of Goethe, Whitman, Emerson, and Melville, they continue up through Proust, Woolf, Nabokov, and Sartre, and then come all the cherished B's—Beckett, Borges, Bernhard, Bolaño—to say nothing of the other 25 letters.

Who carries the torch today? Here's one. Kaul has done a very necessary thing in *A Dream of Horses*, which is to mount a passionate and sensual defense of what literature can do for us explorers of the abyss in these anti-literate, imagistic times. He has not done it in the common way but rather in the best possible. Without drawing a circle between those who find their eyes brightened by the printed word and all the rest of humanity, without fetishizing books and the lifestyle that accompanies them, and, above all, without dwelling on that singularly boring individual known as the author, he has nonetheless penned a very sensitive and intricate investigation of the literary sensibility. "The Light Ascending" begins by describing a man who walks the same path in the mountains over and over again—not a description of a writer, although a description of writer's block if ever there was one. So we are not surprised to find that he *is* a writer, one, in fact, who has received commendation from the great "JC," yet who has not been able to find his way forward. He continues walking his path, until, one night, the path is filled with the music of a flute. Our blocked scribe travels deeper and deeper into the woods until all is lost, and at this moment "I realize I am in a dream, mine or another's, I can't tell." The block has lifted. He finds a cottage bearing JC within and a curious chess game where the knights and bishops have become Beckett, Borges, Faulkner, and Joyce, surrounding the white queen (the muse), the squares around them "the chequered world of art, of joy and despair chasing each other." He and JC continue this game of giving new names to the common symbols surrounding us until the fog lifts "and it feels like I am fast falling into a bottomless pit of darkness." What else can this story be but an elaborate rendition of that sublime sensation conferred when deeply immersed within a dream or a book?

One does not frequently see such a concentration of dreams in a single volume, of characters dropping off to sleep, then coming to with a bolt, murmuring words in the twilight between these states of being, wondering which state they are in. Perhaps we should not be so surprised to see a writer taking stock of that other third of our lives: as Kaul paraphrases Schopenhauer, "dreams and reality are but different chapters of the same book." This preoccupation with the most common liminal experience of them all is, I think, symptomatic of Kaul's fascination with another kind of liminality: the spaces between those names we give to things in this world and the reality they fail to possess. "You can taste the success on your lips," he writes, "but it is only a word spiralling in your head." What a joy it is to discover another of those few writers who really seem to grasp by pure instinct that, for all our righteous mystification of it, language is really just an insufficient means to gutter the flood of sensations assaulting us by the minute. Make no mistake: awareness of language's limits, does not mean diminished ambitions for its use. This is also an author who is steadfastly determined to scrape out a few more feet of consciousness for language to call its turf.

It is a testament to his skill with this clumsy medium of exchange for how often he makes us "taste the success." Though I have never met Kaul, his fiction compels me to believe that he is a person who enjoys the sensual side of life, because he so aptly drizzles throughout these pieces exactly the small pleasures with which the senses persevere between those feasts we arrange for them as a matter of luxury. For instance, the unexpected delight of this salaryman: "The firm was a boutique practice, whatever that means, though it almost always means that you come into money, but not without its dark side—the work filled dark nights. Only when you took a taxi late at night, how you enjoyed the wind making a mess of your hair." Whenever I read that I see a man with the perfectly strict coif mandated by office etiquette closing his eyes in release as it is all undone on some empty highway in a lonely taxi. The hair's loosening becomes his own, his lips part in a silent *ahhhhh*, and for a moment he is a boy again. In short, he lives. Images such as these are the product of a writer for whom words constitute a universe of their own; he has dedicated himself to discovering which ones best defy the black and white of print, which combinations of them will produce the most wonder.

Indeed, it is wonder that guides these seven seekers. One of them says with resignation that "we reach the absurd through different ways," confident, as are all, that we will discover this lackluster prize whether or not we aspire to it. It is not the absurd that these characters fear—for you cannot fear a thing that has grown so wearisome in its commonness—they rather fear that even where absurdity gives way to wonder, wonder will not resolve into truth. A lot to ask, you might say, but then that should give you some idea of the stakes these tales are playing for. To wit: momentarily inhabiting the mind of Beckett, Kaul writes that "the eye cannot truly see until the last tear has been expunged"; if that Irishman who plumbed the absurd so much deeper than we are capable, if he himself finds truth so hard to grasp, then what chance do we stand? Do not despair. Read on. We may not be granted the Truth in *A Dream of Horses*, but we do find some truths: with each story's last word their truths are manifest, all at once we realize that the many points in the sinuous path we have just traced out are not stars but a constellation.

Lastly, it must be said that even though this is not a book that only shares its charms with those who live and breathe for literature, there are particular delights for those who do. In a lovely duet twinning Borges and Beckett into an everlasting stream of recollection, Kaul pauses to linger over their mutual love of Dante:

> Speaking now for the first time since he rowed them out here, he tells of his school copy of Dante with his notes scribbled in the margins from fifty years ago to which he returns whenever he reaches a stasis in his work. Superstitiously, perhaps, he feels he will find there something new to begin. After all, he says in a voice barely perceptible, it was with Dante that it all began. The motion in stasis, and stasis in motion. The moving unmover.
>
> The Comedy, says his companion eagerly, is, of course, the greatest work in all the literatures of the world. In its cosmology, I don't believe for a minute, and yet it is the book I love the most. As for the moving unmover, one may look also at Zeno or the sophist, Gorgias of Lentini, who could well have been behind Kafka.

Look at the movement of these words. From Beckett's discovery of Dante as a schoolboy, to the personal superstition this love grew into, to his sense of the revelation it unleashed, which gives over to Borges's peculiar love for Dante, to his superstition of it, to his own revelation past it. Each time I read these two short paragraphs I laugh in delight at how the laces pull so tightly together and how Kaul has managed to fashion something new from the triangulation of three immortals.

There are many, many other books in *A Dream of Horses*. In fact, we see here a writer brave enough to openly wrestle with his influences, not only in the splendid epigraphs borne at the front of each tale like a torch to light the way, but also in the content of the stories themselves, rife with allusion, name-naming, sidelong glances, and whispered words of thanks. Their enumeration is in keeping with the spirit of openness, of camaraderie, that is so much in evidence throughout this collection. A mention of a few here will perhaps give a better sense of the author than anything else I could say: they include the aforementioned greats, plus John Hawkes, Stendhal, Proust, Carlyle, De Quincey, Novalis, Valéry, Artaud, Schopenhauer . . . There are more, many more, I leave it to you to find them. Your search will be a most joyous one. Turn the page, take a breath, plunge into the delights that await.

SCOTT ESPOSITO

A DREAM OF HORSES

& OTHER STORIES

Parable of the Archer

Gravity is the root of lightness;
stillness, the ruler of movement
Lao-Tzu

The story was told to me by a friend who was leaving for Lhasa the next day. I hadn't heard from him in nearly a year, and here we were, taking shelter in a coffeehouse from the sudden rain that was falling in gusts over the empty streets, making the trees shine like chenille and choking the drains and gutters with muddy water. A spell of silence had come over us, a silence in which thought either collects itself or swiftly melts away. He took a sip from his cup, glanced at the mirror on the far side in which was reflected the blow-up of a girl in an alley between yellow walls, and said, haven't I told you about the parable? It's an old Tao fable. At any rate, I'll tell you again. I can never tire of it. And he spoke thus:

In China of ancient times, there lived an archer who was the ablest among the emperor's great warriors, having won many a battle for the sovereign, annexing one province upon another, and extending the empire to hitherto unknown lands. During a prolonged spell of peace, and for want of a better distraction, he made a formal declaration that any subject of the empire who could prove himself the more skillful in a direct contest could take his place in the royal court and enjoy all the emperor's favours that were earlier his. The contest, the archer announced, would remain open for ten days. Now the archer's fame had travelled far and wide and, as was expected, no match took place. The archer waited in the arena each day only to return at sundown to his palatial quarters and his many wives, filled with a mixed sense of pride and boredom. However, the dawn of the last day brought a visitor who wanted to briefly confer with him. At last a challenger, thought the archer, dressing hurriedly. But what was this, it couldn't be: this submissive, pale-faced, poor villager – empty-handed too!

The villager bowed with unusual grace. When he looked up, a smile flickered on his lip. This troubled the archer. He asked his guest after the purpose of his visit: surely, he wasn't here to take the challenge? Oh, no! Certainly not, sire, answered the villager. There is, however, one who can, he continued, one who is beyond contest, and from what I know I will advise you to not confront him as he will not confront you, for you are no match for him, you will be defeated before you lift your bow. The visitor's words filled the archer with rage, though a curious suspicion was beginning to gnaw at him. Tell me at once who he is, and where will I find him, the archer demanded.

Astride his favourite horse that very morning, the archer headed towards the forest which lay at a two-day trot from the capital. Silence gradually came to fill his hours, and the unending clickety-clack of the horse's hooves made him soporific. Nights were cold and dark and full of falling stars. He ate frugally and slept huddled close to the small fire he had built with his own hands. For the first time in life, he came to feel the magic of simple things. Yet his resolve remained unshaken.

On the third day his eyes saw the ebony mass of the forest covering the horizon and beyond it rising, distant and elemental, the mist-draped mountains. He gave a tug to the horse's reins and dug his heels deeper into its belly, forcing the beast into a gallop. His pride was starting to run in his blood with a renewed vigour and, momentarily, his grip tightened on his bow. Once inside, he forded first a broad and in time a narrow river to find a trail leading to a hut at some distance. The villager had been exact with directions. The archer secured his horse to a tree and continued on foot. Near the hut a man was busy chopping wood. The archer quickly hid behind a tree to observe. Could he be the one? It was inconceivable! Yet there was a certain grace in the axe's movement that betrayed a skilled hand. The archer decided to take a small test. Still concealed from the woodcutter's view, he released an arrow with a gentle pull on the bowstring. But just as the arrow was about to graze the woodcutter's shoulder, it somehow turned back on its course and in the next instant pierced the tree-trunk behind which the archer stood hiding. The woodcutter's movements had been so swift as to be invisible, indeed he was no match to this man's skill. Without even being aware of his adversary, he had defeated him. Free of any desire for a contest, the archer emerged into the clearing and begged the woodcutter to take him as a disciple. The other informed him that whatever he knew about archery he had long since forgotten. The archer was persistent, and at last the woodcutter acquiesced.

For many months the archer remained the woodcutter's pupil, and for many months he did not touch his bow. There were other things he learnt instead: to chop wood free of all effort, aided by the wind, and to catch fish with bare hands, without looking. And little by little awareness of life's movement grew in him. Then one day the woodcutter bade him near and told him he was free to leave, there was nothing more he could offer as a teacher. The archer was astonished to hear this. He had learnt nothing of the only skill that mattered to him. The woodcutter read his thoughts and said, you learn most when you do not learn at all. An arrow is but an arrow, now if you so wish, time itself will turn back on its course. The archer understood, and in that same instant he was aware of the movement of every leaf of every tree, of every bird in the sky, of the fish in water, of earth itself. He knelt before the woodcutter and answered, O Master, your wisdom flows to me, and through your blessing I have become the greatest archer of all.

Can it be? inquired the woodcutter, when the old man of the mountains is still alive. Compared to him my wisdom is but a lark in the sky. These words altered the archer's course. Instead of returning to the capital, he slipped deeper into the forest and having walked for a week reached the mountains. Another day's climb brought him to a tarn where he refreshed himself and rested for the night. Continuing his ascent into the mountains next morning, he presently saw a frail old man, something of a hunchback, slowly descending towards him with an urn balanced on one shoulder. The archer asked him for directions and was shown the way to the cave near the summit. The archer thanked him and resumed his journey.

By noon he had found the cave, which was empty. He decided to wait. It was nearly evening when he saw the old man coming towards him. The archer realized his mistake and made as if to bow. The old man responded with barely a nod, and removed the urn full of water to the ground. Then he looked at the archer's bow and arrows and inquired after their use. The archer was half expecting this. He raised his bow and, taking aim at a bird in flight, shot the arrow. In the next instant it lay quivering at the old man's feet. Oh, this! The old man gave a low grunt. I now recall I too had played like this in my youth. You call this play? asked the archer with some irritation. Wearing a pout on his lip, the old man motioned him to follow. The slate-rock walls of the cave converged behind it and extended beyond the cliff over the ravine which fell thousands of feet below into a white nothingness. The archer followed the old man a few steps, but a cold fierce wind attacked him and he fell to his knees trembling. Just when he was attempting to rise, the elevation produced in him a most terrible vertigo which swiftly brought him back to the ground. The old man, on the other hand, had advanced to the very edge of the rock, and presently he turned to look at the archer. He was poised on his toes, his heels suspended over the ravine. Unmoving like the rock itself, his white silken beard flowing in the wind, he called out to the archer to stand by his side. Frozen with fear, the archer did not reply. Looking up from his low position, he now saw a rare blue rose in the old man's hand. The flower baffled him, and his throat finally felt the warmth of his voice again. O Master, what has a rose to do with archery? The old man was oblivious to the archer's words. Overhead, a flock of swallows was hurrying away in the evening sky. At a glance from the old man, the birds lay twitching on the rock.

Unaware of the tears clouding his vision, the archer saw stretching before him a narrow path at whose end was the rose.

The Passage
(A Scenario)

You gods! My baffled steps are lost in you!
Paul Valéry

The sounds have long fallen into a rhythm. They emerge – from his nostrils, from his hurried step crunching the dry leaves, faintly, from the metal of the rifle slung over his shoulder as it rubs across his khaki shorts, and there is even a jingle from the few bullets in his pocket – cut each other, and lose themselves like flashes in the wide spaces between the trees that are stark and echoless. The heat fails to touch him, for he shivers and his teeth chatter, but his lips are sealed, allowing neither the saline fluids to enter and sting his tongue nor the sobs to escape. Surely this is all a dream, but how to explain the pain that persists in his shoulder and spreads across his back, obliging him to slow down every now and then. Yet he must keep up his pace; from what he knows of these parts, the brook is at least two miles away.

Barely a year ago, he was still in the village, playing, running errands, and going to the new school. Although not quite taken in by school, he was the last to leave each day, for he had early on made the discovery of some books in the common room where it was always cool and shady. These were strange things, alive to the touch, and he stayed alone, reading and weaving fantasies until light began to leave the sky. He was just beginning to make sense of the words, but the pictures spoke to him openly – of distant lands and times, fishlike maidens and fire-spitting dragons, magic cloaks and tunnels you took to slip into the earth's belly. Only if he had not been hurriedly despatched to live with his uncle in town. More than once, his family had received feelers from the guerrillas that he was now old enough to handle a gun.

In town he could not go to school immediately: that he had to wait for the term to end was one in many reasons. With each day he grew ever more listless and six months later succumb to the offer of becoming a soldier in a new 'civil resistance' movement fostered by the authorities. The allowance was handsome and at last the bookstore lay within easy reach. But without a warning he was removed to the camps on the edge of the forest along the main road to guard the town and resist the advance of the guerrillas. Here all you saw were khaki clothes, guns and bullets, and some food, but never books. Here, too, was a boy of his age who by the third month had become his friend.

Last evening he had found his friend fingering – he could not believe it – a book, hardly outside his grasp, waiting. He moved towards it, but just then there was a shuffle of steps outside the tent and, as if a trance had been broken, he ran away in confusion, though not before hurriedly imploring his friend to bring the book along in the morning to their secret place. Night was spent counting stars, awaiting the light that would wipe them away. At dawn he was already at the meeting point in the forest, though nearly three hours passed before his friend showed up – he could not comprehend it – empty-handed. Uncontrollable rage welled up in him, making him dizzy, and he came to himself only when he heard the shot.

He falls into the stream with open arms and drinks greedily, never noticing the shadows that are thickening over the hill.

The Light Ascending

All will grow dark again.
Samuel Beckett

Somewhere behind the tall water tank is the trail that leads into the forest. The iron mesh has an opening there, like a wound that hasn't been allowed to heal, and you can slip past it to the other side without any discomfort. Locals who work at the institute prefer this shorter course to return home every evening. Part of the way they leave the trail to cleave the wilds, descending into the bowl of the valley through routes that remain hidden to the untrained eye, routes as many as rivulets in the rain, routes like hieroglyphs that can only be traced if one learns to read the symbols, to touch and to look closely: the impress on a patch of grass, the carelessly crushed cigarette butt, the broken twig, the startled call of a bird in flight.

At nine thousand feet above the sea, this is pine country. Leaving the stinking dump that Simla has become – a dump through which remnants of the Raj rise like smoke here and there, not just vertically through space, but horizontally, too, along the axis of time, moving from a subdued and painful past towards a cataclysmic future – and travelling for an hour on the road that spirals higher and higher, you come into these hills that have not yet been laid waste by progress. Here, deep in the pines and deodars, tall and dark and indistinguishable at a distance from each other, magic survives and magical events have a chance to occur.

From the guest quarters of the institute, it is barely a fifty-step walk up the incline to the water tank which stands on a high wrought-iron structure. Around it there is some flat space to move about and enjoy the vista that opens up between the trees. At dawn, before the smoke and haze has obliterated the view, one can see the snowy peaks, blue, pink, and orange at once, that girdle the world's edges.

Yet by noon there is little solitude here, so one ventures past the iron mesh in search of it and the mud path mercifully takes him where he belongs. First it ascends, then curves, and later begins to descend, only to flatten and meander under the canopy of branches. To either side the forest slopes downwards and, intermittently, one can glimpse the road that clasps the hill like a snake, hundreds of feet below. In time the trail splits, one part dropping slightly, skirts along the hill and at half a mile's walk ends at the spa resort, the other rises to the hill's crest where an old water pumping station awaits the solitude-seeker.

On coming to know of the *strawberry trail*, I decided to explore it and thought of going to the resort at least once before my money, whatever little I had of it, ran out. So I set forth one morning soon after my arrival. In barely a half hour I could see the cone-like slate-blue roofs of the building rising over the trees. Suddenly the road bent sharply to the left and the view was lost behind the hill. Now the road was entirely under its shadow and the pines acquired a blackish hue, but above the sky was high and clear and dazzling, all of it making a very pretty picture.

Unlike in life, mountains always propel me to choose the course that moves upwards. Thus I instinctively selected the narrow path rising past young twisted pines and shrubs whose names I did not know, when it was apparent that the wider, flatter, oft-trodden road I had left behind was the correct way. But as in life so in the hills there is compensation for the drifter.

The pumping station was in a state of disrepair, and yet there was something striking about it. I went around in circles, unable to pinpoint it. On one side was a line of ancient trees, interspersed with a few young poplars. Here I sat down and was suddenly tired, not just by the slight trek, but with the burden of my choices that lay heavy on me and were now turning into an almost physical sensation of pain. Every story demands some insight into the life of its characters, and one could not have asked for a quieter setting than in which I found myself to recall past events.

Floating in and out of the courts, I had reached the point from where I could simply stare at myself, ten, twenty, thirty years into the future: a Dantean vision that unsettled me each time. At twenty-six, with much difficulty and late-night hardships, I had written a novel whose publication I had part financed upon it being turned down by several publishers. Aside from winning a small prize and some readers, it went unnoticed. As was also apparent, it made me little money. And yet there was a singular result: I started corresponding with JC, the best of them all, the writer *par excellence*, decorated everywhere, yet miraculously aloof, private, and dignified. Less a writer than a monk. The legend of how fiercely he guarded his privacy refused to die; indeed the talk resurfaced each time he failed to appear to collect a prominent international prize. Obviously I did not know his whereabouts, so I sent a copy of my novel to his agent in London. To my surprise, I received a brief remark about the book inside of a month from some obscure town in Australia. I was elated. I wrote again and in response received a personally autographed copy of one of his novels with a short letter in longhand in which he told me that I would write many books and that I should never worry about criticism. Kind of him to have written that, but criticism was the least of my worries then and counts for nothing now that I am amid this solitary beauty.

Two years later, I departed from the city. I had not left much behind, whatever few relationships I had cherished were already on a downward spiral.

An almost unbearable cawing filled the air. I awoke to find a raven, its black plumage glossy in the noon light, perched on the tap which jutted out from a wall of the pumping station, watching me. Every once in a while, there was the sound of a lorry passing on the road below or maybe it was just the wind swaying the pines. Later, seated above the evergreen forest, the chain of snow peaks obscured by distance and yet transmitting their solid presence, I ate an expensive meal in the open, returning light in the pocket but feeling all the better for it.

It's three weeks since my arrival. I have made several trips to the pumping station, and two even to the resort. For hours I read or lie under the trees gazing at the sky where at times I can detect a few old faces – always happy faces – in the shapes of clouds. The forest has its own music, clear, simple, and fluid; it glides over you like a stream in which you have fallen with joyous abandon. Choices, however, remain. And time.

*

The sky is a riot of stars. I sip my drink and let it trickle down my throat, absorbing its warmth. The wind is sharp and chilly and makes me yearn for the fiery sky. It flows over the hillside and the giant trees tremble in it, a roar erupts that drowns every other sound. Yet before the wind has risen again, I can hear very faintly the notes of a flute.

The notes grow prominent and I realize with a slight jolt that I am already in the forest, lured by the melody. At first the notes are spaced out like droplets, but soon they merge and rise into a river of hope and longing. Unbeknown to me, I have made the choice. Now all that remains is to walk the path to its end. Fortunately, the moonshine filters through the overhanging branches, and I have followed this path many times in the day. Still I cannot make out at once when I hit the fork. The music is coming not from above, but from the side of the hill, from the direction of the resort.

The trail stretches endlessly ahead. Even after half an hour, I am no closer to my destination. Either time has slowed down or I have somehow lost my way. I am deep in the forest; here the moonshine does not reach me, but countless tiny eyes follow my steps in the dark. The music has stopped too, it occurs to me. Then the moon tears away from a cloud and I see at last the familiar green gate. Beyond it, however, I see nothing. This is when I realize I am in a dream, mine or another's, I can't tell.

A glade. Pale clouds of mist roll across it in files, while above sparks of an exploding universe emphasize the dense silhouettes of trees that make its circumference – how calm they appear from a distance. A vague smell of burnt wood rests on the air and I walk in its direction. Then I see a cottage in the distance, streaks of smoke are coming off its chimney. A few old cedars close the view from one end. Suddenly I am standing at its door, on each side a paper lantern producing a velvety glow, about to knock. Hairs rise on my arms and the back of my neck, and I know I am going to meet a ghost from the past.

I knock twice and wait. After a time, I knock again. I hear a lumbering, approaching step. The door creaks, and what I see – or cannot see at first – is a curious blue light in which I do not instantly recognize his face. He says nothing, only stands aside for me to enter. Most of the room is in shadow, but gradually my eyes adjust to the light coming from the window and from the embers in the grate. Under the window, there is a round table with two chairs. In the funnel of light, I see a chessboard on which only five pieces remain. Clearly this is not a game in progress, for both the kings are missing from the board. The board itself is placed diagonally such that a corner points at the player. At its centre stands a white queen, bishops and knights surrounding her in a rhombus-like formation. For some strange reason, I silently start burdening them with names: 'the black bishop – Borges; the white knight – Joyce; the black knight – Faulkner; the white bishop . . .'

'Beckett,' his voice down to a whisper reaches me. By the time I turn, he has settled in one of the chairs.

'Beckett,' I repeat, hearing my voice for the first time and taking the empty chair. His face, silhouetted against the blue light, appears to be young and timeless. 'And the queen?' I ask.

'. . . isn't the queen, of course. Just like this isn't chess.'

'Who's she, then? The Muse? And this, the chequered world of art, of joy and despair chasing each other?'

'Chess is a proof that we live in a world of symbols, a world which we both pinch and populate.'

'What are books then,' I inquire.

'What they've always been, rivers, stars, galaxies.' He has moved deeper into his chair and his lean frame is completely in the dark. He is his voice alone, though I can't tell if this voice belongs to him, for I haven't heard it before. 'What do you think music is?'

'A bridge,' I say instinctively. 'From one void to the next.' I have a vague feeling that he is smiling. I am enjoying the game now, and I go on: 'What is poverty a symbol of?'

'The avarice of the rich,' the voice answers. With horror I understand that I am losing my way in a labyrinth of symbols, where everything is a symbol for everything else, a web that may hold me prisoner forever. Suddenly, on an inspiration, I ask: 'What does the calm ironic smile of a child symbolize?'

My voice echoes around me. The chair opposite me is empty. But I know the answer. I say the word softly to myself.

The word weighs me down, gives me vertigo. Light begins to

fade from the room and return to the sky, and the room begins to spin, and it feels like I am fast falling into a bottomless pit of darkness.

A Dream of Horses

his mind was a turmoil of words and fancies, incomplete fancies and insufficient words, but already he knew that this and only this was the reality of his life.
Vladimir Nabokov

In the autumn of that year you could do nothing but look at the sky for long spells and think how glad you were to be alive. The wind that rose from the river behind the old fort was cool as it broke over the green expanse of the public gardens only to rise a second time to quiver the high branches of the pines and silver oaks planted in several groves and of the trees that stood tall and proud marking the gardens' circumference and lining the main avenue. Much higher above blew a different wind, twisting and turning clouds into fantastic shapes. The sun was brilliant and tender, emphasizing the blueness of the sky that was everywhere.

We breathe in the present, but are alive only in retrospect, in a time long lost to that treacherous monster: memory. For to be alive is to be happy and sad at the same time, to be unable to tell one from the other, to merely feel a faint melancholy beauty in your heart; a happiness aware of sadness, beauty of a joy girdling its despair. And, at best, each of us can only *re-live* this beauty, for the present is past so soon. Now that I lie here recuperating from an illness whose causes and effects may never be entirely known to me, I think it was in the autumn of that year when I was truly alive.

Many things began that autumn which, it seems, have not yet reached a conclusion I could call desirable. But things one desires take time to happen, and sometimes they do not happen at all. Other things happen instead. Not necessarily better or worse, merely different from those that one awaits with much hope and fervour. Limited that our understanding is of the many causes that beget a life and sustain it through its modest time of activity, one may be tempted to describe this as absurd. Close to the middle of the century just past, it was this theme of the *absurd* that had become such a vogue in the arts that no painter or writer could remain apathetic to it. Musicians, too, generously employed it to create unheard of, beguiling tunes in the avant-garde cafés of New York and Paris, and the other more fashionable ones overlooking the Mediterranean on either side. Verily, it had all begun at the turn of the century when 'time', with a truth found only in numbers, was shown to stretch or contract like a rubber band. A decade or two later, a group of physicists in Copenhagen had shocked those who were willing to be shocked by declaring that the smallest particles in the universe exist in multiple states simultaneously until we choose to observe one to the exclusion of others, thus rupturing the belief in a single coherent reality, and thereby pushing physics into the realm of metaphysics, and opening science, in a manner of speaking, to conjecture. While modern science continued its bold attempts to prod the layers of reality, it was the war, like all wars, which finally settled the matter, at least philosophically, in favour of the *absurd* . . . But how did I get to this? Surely this wasn't my intention. I ask your indulgence for once. You must understand that I have not put pen to paper in nearly four years – I who had long ago sworn to live only by this one joy. Even now my hand isn't steady as it exerts itself to catch up with my thoughts, possessed that they are with a whim of their own. My malady being an old one – not due to the passage of time, but in fact due to its complete absence from my side – and having not left me entirely, I often succumb to the temptation of random thoughts. In time I hope to be cured of this indiscipline – as I have been cured of others, I am told, in these past years – so that I may again write a clear, coherent prose. For the present, allow me to continue, and I promise to rein in my thoughts whenever they take to a gallop.

At that time in my life, I lived in the basement of a house located in a quiet neighbourhood just across the main avenue from the public gardens. Three stories high, the structure confessed a slight Moorish influence, particularly in the curved balconies that were in turn enhanced by the black wrought-iron balustrades supported on curling balusters. The windows were large and minimalistic in design. By noon the cream-coloured façade took on a flushed look, but its lines became sharper still. In front of the house was a small, well-tended garden, bounded by a five-feet-high hedge.

Beneath this colossal mass of stone was a room crowded with a green-striped camelback sofa, two wicker chairs, a writing desk, a low square table, a bed with stout, tiny wheels underneath, a dark wood armoire with a long mirror affixed to its door, and a chest of drawers of the same dark wood as the armoire. In two of the corners were lanterns attached to iron stands which, when switched on, filled the room with a soft golden light. Four long shelves that jutted out of a wall held all my books. There was hot water in the bathroom, and a bathtub in which you could go to sleep without straining your neck. The glass windows were square and wide, stretching from the ceiling to a third of the room's height, letting in a lot of light. In the night you could see the stars, and on some nights even the moon. How distant it all seems, now coming to haunt me like a fluid dream!

To this room I had come just a few months after finishing my studies, coming with very little besides clothes and books. A week or two later I started work at a firm of solicitors, select in its clientele and practice, priding itself in advising banks and lending institutions to sell stocks, bonds, and other fancy hybrids of big and small companies in trading exchanges inside and outside the country. The firm was a boutique practice, whatever that means, though it almost always means that you come into money, but not without its dark side – the work filled dark nights. Only when you took a taxi late at night, how you enjoyed the wind making a mess of your hair.

Some months later, I went to visit a friend in London, and together we travelled to France, Paris, and then down to the Mediterranean coast, where the cool breeze mingles with a brightness that dazzles everything under it, and you see the expanse of water that separates you from that land where the sun covers everything in a silvery haze, neglected, rich and poor at once, its deep forests with animals jumping in them, its never-ending wastes, its broad muddy rivers, its blood-red sunsets, its brown, rugged mountains with open mouths laced with snow, and its people that seem to grow from the very earth like a shrub or a root – nowhere else did nature reveal itself so free of hesitancy as in Africa. I itched to cross the sea and walk on that old land, what if only to graze the tip of Morocco or the quays of Alexandria. Such a romantic notion! What will my convalescent imagination not conjure up! But it doesn't take long to find one's burden again (these words have come to trouble me; I have taken to the habit of turning them over and over in my head. They aren't mine for sure. To whom then do they belong? A poet? A philosopher? A longshoreman? It comes to the same thing): my leave was at an end, and I had to get back to do what I didn't like much. Before returning, however, I spent a quiet day in Paris walking around the city, where, in one of its gardens, perhaps Tuileries, I saw with amazement how an old man, holding the slender stem of a yellow chrysanthemum between his teeth (images, so many images!), fed several sparrows from his outstretched hands, breadcrumbs between the thumb and the index finger, sparrows perched on his arms and shoulders and all around him. In that moment of revealed beauty, there rose up in me the feeling that something was about to happen, that my life was about to slip through a magic chute.

Then I found myself at Montmartre, outside the Basilique du Sacré-Cœur, breathing deep in the wind that rose suddenly, as if at my bidding, having risen from the forests outside Paris, or perhaps from further down, from the sea itself, or coming down at a terrible speed from the mountains in the north, or even from a neglected, frozen arm of the Ganges, or it was the air from another time that had somehow picked up the current of life after having remained dormant for centuries, for even that is possible: I took in the whole of Paris, first the light haze trailing over the city, which in no time had become a whirlwind taking everything with it, from the river, the earth, and the trees, to those colossal structures of stones and columns, all the iron of the Eiffel, the very flesh and thoughts of its constituent beings, but which once inside, instantly turned to all vapours, rising in spirals to no fixed destination, moving for months, for years maybe, until I could wrestle with it no more, this demon that it had become, so sly and rebellious, and spewed it all out on the page, where it would take form once more, inch by inch, as one word crept under the shadow of another, a city that repeated itself endlessly in forever-new patterns. And then I opened my eyes and Paris lay beneath me unaware of my presence.

How many months I worked at the firm upon my return? Seven, perhaps eight. Finally I was free to do as I pleased. If I lived sparingly, my savings could last two years. Why, I was not the first one to do so. Joyce had done it for his art so shamelessly – all artists do so, in their own brave or shameless ways. Countless noble examples were there. I will do it as well. And I will beat them all at it. They make me smile, these last words. The pride of youth! And yet it is not incorrect to say that all great art begins in a thought of vanity.

On that autumn day, walking to the bookshop in the neighbourhood, I could hear the wind go about its business in the eucalyptuses with a dry crackling sound. Crows perched on telephone poles and the wires linking them, clutching countless conversations in their claws which escaped through their claws all the same as the crows stood still and the world spun beneath them and they with it.

I was there in no time. The market at that hour always appeared deserted – hardly a market it was, beginning and ending with a grocery store; between these: a store that sold antique furniture, the local branch of a bank, a small bakery, a post office, a large showroom with black mannequins in windows dressed in white lacy fabrics, empty on most days, a shop selling sports equipment, two or three stores with their shutters always down, and finally that beautiful book shop with a ceiling made up entirely of mirrors and a floor that pleasantly creaked under your step.

Across from the market sat on a low stool the florist who at that moment was busy sprinkling water over the flowers with measured jerks of his arm, water that he collected in the hollow of his hand, with fingers curled in the traditional style, from a half-broken pail. The owner of the newsstand followed his movements closely for want of a better distraction while cracking peanuts by pressing them between his thumb and forefinger and removing the contents to his mouth with an absent habitual air.

Bending away from the world and its impressions, I sauntered towards the bookstore, towards the distant and elemental worlds of books, worlds that language alone can forge. Nearby some children were playing hopscotch, clapping and hooting and making a racket. Watching them at their game, a vague uneasiness came over me, as if dark sinister events were lurking round the corner, ready to pounce on me like a pack of burglars. My head full of such thoughts I entered the store, where I did not instantly notice the girl who came to mean so much to me for so little a time. Oh, Sevica, only if . . .

My thumb aches. No, my hand and arm too. It is getting cold. The mountains are collecting shadows for the night to spread them about. I must rest for the day. How easily I tire. How difficult it seems to move your pen to shape words, sentences, stories. It has become a labour, a mere physical activity. And yet I have not written, no, scribbled, more than a handful of lines. So much the better to roll words and sentences in your memory, where they float calmly and because they are formless always retain some element of truth.

*

In the autumn of that year you first made his acquaintance, and by spring he was gone, taken away, removed to higher, lighter climes, for his situation, as was plainly evident, had deteriorated. What all can a cycle of seasons contain! But before that period of strange and spectacular happenings, the years are banked with fog, so distant it seems: your return from Moscow during the summer, and the harsh winter earlier, harsher still for your mother's soul hadn't yet taken your leave, lingering over the frozen river and coming to wait on you in those long white nights. You had finished college, and were awaiting your father's change of term at the Foreign Office so you could be homebound with him and your sister. You wept in your sleep and sleep-walked through the days, at times simply standing by the window and contemplating for hours the blue- and green-striped bulbous domes of the cathedral. You read and you played the piano, something for which you didn't have much talent, but even to your dazed, suffering mind, Tchaikovsky now sounded more like Tchaikovsky, Brahms and Debussy clearer echoes of their selves, and with each bar, each piece, her soul hovered a little higher until one day at last it flew off. Soon the Moskva began to flow, the sky cleared, trees turned green and birds shook their feathers in them. You took to walking along the river and almost always ended at a bench in the Alexander Garden, behind you the yellow and ochre wall of the Kremlin rising steeply like a precipice.

Eventually you came home, pulling autumn along. The wind picked up and the earth breathed again putting a spring in your step. Cottony clouds cantered away in the sky and dry leaves purred in empty drains. You resumed your walks and in the public gardens across the main avenue, in the silence within and without, rose up the myriad voices of the season. With each day you played better, a lightness pervaded your touch that suggested the soul's flight.

Early one evening you were at the bookstore to select a gift for your father's birthday. Maybe this slight gesture will break the spell of silence and suffering over him and unite the three of you in your loss. How happy you were to locate Stendhal's *Armance*, one of his favourites, a copy of which you had misplaced some years ago. It saddened you now to recall how he hadn't even noticed its loss, for time had made him a different man. Perhaps the book will bring back the totemic power of literature in his life, and perhaps he will embrace you – isn't that what you ever wanted? How much of the child was still there in you?

The bell-chime announced a visitor. And you looked up and you saw him. His gaze did glide over you, but you knew he had not seen. You were straight in his line of vision and he had not seen. You looked down and you looked up again. There was something in those eyes: a wandering sadness that at last has found a place to settle down. You could see that. Of course, it wasn't just this as you know now; even then his mind had been struggling against the evil lure of its own terrible designs.

But the next moment he was smiling, his gaze fixed on you, no, not on you, on something near you. It was the Stendhal you had carelessly left on the counter while thumbing through another book. At first you wanted to claim it from his cheerful stare; yet you stood unmoving. Something in you wanted to prolong the happy state in that stranger.

This was not to be, for now he finally saw you and at once a curtain of boredom fell on his eyes. Awhile he moved to the pull of books, picking one or another, glancing through them, lingering on them and, more than once, you thought, contemplating a book's price longer than necessary. At last, a book in hand, he withdrew to the shop's inner courtyard. You paid and collected the Stendhal and drifted towards the door, a part of you not wanting to leave. Thrusting the glass-door into the world you stepped out and, instantly, from the eucalyptus across the road, its leaves a pale green in the evening light, several crows sticking to it like on an impressionist canvas cawed a few times in chorus. This was all the motivation you needed. Falling back gladly into the shop, you coolly walked over to the courtyard to confront the fellow.

He sat on the only bench, lost in the movement of clouds, bulbous and full of light in this moment, unaware of your approaching step. Indifferently yet expertly, he was spreading tobacco on a piece of fine paper, his fingers busy curling it around into a cigarette. He appeared a little dazed, like a sailor on a leave of absence, slightly unsure on land, of its deceits and mercies. A novel of John Hawkes lay neglected at his side, concealing under it a classic. Now he saw you, and his smile was at once shy and inviting, feeding your confidence. He removed the books to the other side and you sat down beside him.

He offered that apology for a cigarette to you, but you shook your head, saying, no-thank you. So he put the cigarette to his lip, lit it with a match and puffed at it a few times, blowing out smoke like the spouts of a whale. For sometime he didn't take any note of you, and you thought, what an incredible thing to do, sitting here, watching the fellow lost to daydreams. Then all at once he turned and, with an openness that both surprised and eased you, inquired if you'd walk with him to the nearby bakery for a coffee.

There, sitting round a table with a plastic top, taking sips from the paper cups, you finally got talking: that, as things had come to pass, he cared only for books and you were beginning to feel a certain touch for music. He nodded like he had always known this, though he knew nothing then. Extracting the tobacco pouch from a pocket in his denims, he waited. So on you went about music, about the Moscow summer (to which he sighed, ah, Moscow!) and, for no reason whatever, you opened to him the anguish of your mother's demise. He sat very still, rolling yet another of his cigarettes, until your thoughts started to spin a little, in time alighting on him, expectancy shinning in your eyes. He saw it this time, quite clearly, and vaguely at first he spoke of *Armance*, that in this city it was rare to find a girl reading Stendhal, that it was in fact the book in your hand which made it easy for him to talk to you (didn't you approach him first?), that he was at present reading Chinese poetry (he spoke something about Li-Po's poems), that you were the girl of his dreams if you could play the cello or the violin as well, and, if so, it would follow that life itself was a dream or a web of dreams. Laughter gurgled in his throat, yet it was you who gave it an outlet; the poor chap had forgotten how to. You said you didn't play either of the two but only the piano, and although you didn't play it all that well you would be happy for him to judge that day after the morrow.

He came punctually at six-thirty. The bell pealed through the corridor and you knew it was him. You saw him from the window upstairs, wearing a blue-striped shirt, freshly laundered and creased in places due to negligent ironing, and slate-grey trousers, hands behind his back, hair slightly wet from the shower. You opened the door and ushered him in. He tiptoed into the living room where you suddenly turned to look at him. He smiled and his hand now held a gift for you: a book of poems by Ingeborg Bachmann. You had never read any poetry by her and you told him as much. He said her poems were beautiful and a flicker of longing crossed his eyes. Observing him it occurred to you that he was going to lose in the end, it was written all over him, that the world would defeat him simply with its indifference, and he would fall, poor soul, thinking himself a silent hero, of his noble sacrifice, whereas in truth it would come to nothing. How foolish this was, all of it, all the silly emotions one gradually amassed against a universe which, in its empyrean wisdom, remained forever silent. And you wanted there and then to hold him to yourself, to tell him that you would play to him, listen to him, even love him if need be, anything to make the sinking easier or less painful. Wasn't that all one could do for another? Unable to free yourself from such thoughts, you suddenly took a step closer and embraced him. His arms closed about you; his touch on your skin was icy, and a tremor of unease passed over you, for his blood was freezing inside him.

He thought he could spare the courtesies now that you were friends and, pointing to the bar, asked for some whiskey. You removed your father's decanter from the shelf and poured a measure of it in a glass. Ice? Two cubes. You handed him the glass and walking over to the piano, said to yourself, quick, quick, gulp it down old boy, let it warm you, and for goodness' sake let it take away that bluish hue from under your eyes. But he simply stood against the wall at the far end, stirring the ice cubes in his glass with a finger. Oh, how cold, you thought, how very cold! And knowing not how to help began with a little-known piece by Scarlatti.

Soon you met him again, then again and again. One day in the park, reclining on the grass, he spoke about his meeting with an old man who sat cross-legged, pulling butterflies out of his mouth one after the other. He did have, he mused, something Nabokovian in him. Hearing this your lips spread into a downward curve, a slight foreboding filling your chest, but he was calm like he had narrated a plain fact for anyone to see. His wandering gaze had come to rest on the stone mausoleums, covered in the melancholy of a lost era. Countless pigeons ruptured it here and there with the songliness of their short circular flights. Now he looked at you and the expression in your eyes made him sigh. Thereupon swiftly forgetting the matter he smiled. In no time the air was abuzz with excitement as a group of children came running towards the two of you, and in tow came a huge pink-and-blue balloon, the first of the rally, sailing over the trees.

Having asked after his writing many a time, you at last succeeded and he showed you one of his poems. He said it was about a girl in a blue mackintosh running away from a shadow in pursuit, about the impressive curve of her dress within, bunched at the waist, and the warm wet night without. You read it later, once, twice, and then once more, failing to make much sense of it. For unless he had meant it as a joke, the poem he spoke about existed only in some shadowy corner of his mind or was completely concealed by the words it was draped with. You didn't tell him so, and he didn't seem particularly eager to hear your opinion of it.

Rolling through the endless fields of freedom, how we yearn for bondage. Something to stop the water like flow, something to bind and contain us: a piece of land providing the warmth of repetition, a vista that fills us with longing each time, the obsessive lure of possessions, cul-de-sacs of desire, the sanctum of art. Anything will do, nearly anything to fill this dizzying emptiness of the heart, to weigh it down.

With what startling simplicity he had entered your life, bringing to it, all of a sudden, the sizzling swing of jazz, which could only go one way: to the concluding crash of the cymbal. Dtisssshhhhh . . . Love came between you, a love fluid and resilient like water, love that still flows between you, never mind the expanding space and the contracting time. These are but small matters . . .

Winter had silently sneaked in. Your step was brisk as you walked to his quarters on that never-to-be-forgotten December evening. The hunter had come up in the sky, hands and feet in position, ready to strike yet frozen for eternity in the glare of some unhappy god. Your thoughts moved round him, circled that life which was fabulous just as it was ordinary. Having not seen him in three days, you were eager to reach your destination. How long it seemed from the night he had lain in bed with you discussing his unwritten book on chess, ripe in the head, ready to jump out. The talk about Duchamp, Miguel de Unamuno, and the ancient Hindu myths was still with you. In what childlike frenzy he had spoken; and yet behind all the glitter of ideas, his mind had been for long choking.

Entering through the side gate of the lawn, you saw the glow from the windows, and your heart leapt from its place as if it was the first time. Bending your knees you'd crouch on the ground to observe him a moment. Then, maybe you'd tap on the glass with your foot to announce your arrival. . . But where was he? You waited. No sign of him, no movement. . . Oh, how stupid of you to not see it right away! A part of his arm limply hung from the sofa. Quickly descending the steps, you were just about to press the bell when you saw that the door was ajar. Soundlessly you entered and bolted the door behind you. Moving near him, a vague suspicion rising with every step, your sight fell on the table littered with a half-empty bottle of Jameson, four or five books, a writing pad, and a chessboard. He lay sprawled on the sofa, whispering in his sleep. You could see his breath for a cold draught had filled the room. A better part of the blanket had slipped from his legs to the ground, putting a shiver in his mumbling. Puffing out your cheeks, you bent towards him to hear better. *See . . . Dick seeks . . . not . . . It is . . . madly see . . . him* . . . At first it made no sense, but then you saw among the books on the table, *Moby-Dick*, and the vision was astonishing in its clarity, making you fear for him (. . . *brr* . . . *the water's cold* . . . *far* . . . *far* . . .) for he was chasing the phantom of his own ruin, not in the balmy tropics but in the ice-worlds of the pole (perhaps because he was cold). You came nearer still and covered his trembling lips with your own, and he gladly surrendered to their warmth. Soon his arms had slipped past your waist through the open coat and his hand was rubbing your hip. You raised your head a little and, magnetically, his head too moved upwards. Unable to find what he was searching with his lips, he opened his eyes. For a few moments he was still, his vacant gaze resting on the tiny silver elephant dangling in the shadow of your chin. Then, without a word, he rose to his feet and, lifting you from the waist, your legs clasped around him, carried you over to the bed. There, with your head hanging from the edge and your thighs wrapped tight around his midriff, his flesh quickly came to life, warm and responsive to your every move, every caress, anticipating your thoughts and doing their bidding. Tears dropped to your eyes and, through the open window, you saw the hunter stir in the starry forest of the night sky.

Presently you were roused from your sleep by the chill of the wind on your back, waking up on top of him. You rolled down to his side, pulling over the blanket at once. He didn't move, like he was in a deep sleep, though in truth he was wide-awake and murmuring about the horses.

Phantom Days

in this world, beauty is so common
Jorge Luis Borges

Again I wake up with the sound of drums in my ears, the mattress hard under me. I bury my face in the crook of my arm that is on the pillow, while with the other hand I search for the watch. The drums seem nearer now; their beats ruffle the hair on the back of my head and slide down into my ears, but sleep has not left me entirely and it is with difficulty that I lift my head to check the time. It is not yet eight and I have already twice repeated these movements in the last twenty minutes, which could well be three hours. Then all at once the beating of drums ceases. The company has concluded its morning march. A bugle is heard three times. After that all is silent, though I now become aware of another sound, that of the old fan rotating above. Fighting the urge to fall back to sleep I turn around and rub my eye with a finger. I can think of nothing as I follow the movements of the fan through the mosquito net that closes on me from all sides – like a room within a room. In my sleep I recall feeling the warmth of a body. But here I lie alone, ignoring the discomfort of a full bladder. I see the road that passes through the forest, its trees yellowish-brown skeletons, their branches bare and rising willy-nilly towards a sky which is white with heat; the earth as far as you can look is covered with dead leaves. It is a landscape at the end of time.

At last I rise from the bed and go over to the bathroom. The floor tiles are dirty with shoe marks. I spot a lizard trying to escape through a hole in the roof. Back in the room, I greedily gulp down all the water in the bottle on the table. Next to it is a flask from which I pour coffee in one of the two cups in the tray – a sweet milky syrup that I can't bear to finish. Through the window comes a breeze that is cool, but outside the meadows are dry and dusty, and would resemble a desert were it not for the pines that break the monotony here and there – of a green that makes them look like silhouettes. It has not rained in two years. I try to think of my last visit, but the view is so desolate that no memories come to mind. Instead a sudden dizziness rises to my head.

The door is not bolted. I step into the gallery (that circumscribes this L-shaped, single-storey building), and instinctively look around for monkeys. There are two kinds of them in this place. Those with a silver fur and black faces are quite well-behaved, my friend often feeds them chickpeas from his hand. The other ones are pink-bottomed rogues, not afraid to bite or claw on the flimsiest of pretexts. For some reason neither is present today. Wind that rises now and then curls the branches of the trees in the yard, and pushes the leaves on the ground first to one side and then to the other, forming and eroding strange continents. I sit down on the steps at the edge of the gallery, my arms on my knees. The sun is getting stronger and warms my shins that ache slightly from all the walking. It will be another hot day even though this town of all but ten thousand is a hill resort in the middle of the country, for these hills are old and low, content to merely watch over the forests stretching in all directions, never rising to mighty heights.

Sounds on the tiled roof make me stand. A mischievous one

jumps from the edge of the roof on to the iron gate and in two leaps is already on the other side of the mud path where it quickly climbs up a mango tree. A stone swishes past me and hits the trunk. My friend appears from the other end of the yard, swinging, to my surprise, a slingshot on a finger. He is back from his morning run; all these days he has been regular about it. Running helps him keep his asthma in control, he says, yet at home he can do so only on weekends, morning being the only time when he reads his court briefs. When only a few steps away, he tosses the slingshot at me. I manage to catch it with one hand and, for a moment just as he is entering the room, stare at the back of his t-shirt which is damp with sweat. In the past week we have become accustomed to the silence of this place and, though we talk for hours sometimes, we have learnt to do without courtesies.

A slingshot. I do not know how to use it. Like all else it requires a certain skill in handling, and I am not particularly good at cultivating skills. In school, we often rolled bits of paper into pellets and hit each other using a rubber band stretched between the thumb and the index finger as a slingshot. Even at that I fared poorly. However, this is a more sophisticated instrument. I observe it closely – the fork is a perfect Y made of solid wood and the sling is of soft leather, two blue rubber tubes making the connexion – but then I get bored and decide to practice my aim. Picking up a few pebbles, I shoot them in air. At first the stones travel only a short distance, but with the seventh or eighth one I manage to clear the yard and lose it in the branches of a tree where it releases a dry crackle. I see a monkey watch me from behind the iron gate, perhaps the same one which had earlier climbed the tree. I play at taking aim but even before I can steady the pebble it has bounded off.

The caretaker arrives with our breakfast. It consists of toasts and eggs and tea brewed with ginger flakes in it. He is a small fellow with a childlike smile that never leaves his face and puts a twinkle in his eyes, his short hair covers his head like a mat. I ask him to bring a pitcher of cold water.

Inside, my friend has pulled up the mosquito net from his part of the bed and is sitting cross-legged smearing butter on his toast. I sit there sipping the tea that leaves a delicious gingery sting on the palate, and ask him if he was able to make the call. No, he tells me, the kiosk hadn't yet opened for the day. The caretaker enters carrying the pitcher of water, asks what he should prepare for lunch. My friend asks him to repeat the menu of the day before – curry, yellow lentils, and rice, but I feel little appetite for lunch.

After breakfast, my friend picks up the slingshot that is lying on the table and goes out into the yard to shoot stones. I lie down in bed and stare at the teak wood ceiling painted a deep brown. Sleep hovers in the room, but I have learnt a few tricks to avoid it, one of them being not to read while lying down. So instead I think of the past.

My friend comes in, says it will rain, pointing, beyond the roof, at the cliff which is partly in shadow. Indeed clouds have flown over the sun and the wind has freshened. But they look nothing like rain clouds to me. All the same it is good weather to be in the open. So we carry a chair each from the room and put them under the tree that has a cement platform round its trunk.

The wind strokes me in a million places, enfolds me. The chair next to me is empty; the book he has been reading is lying upside down on it. He is up on the platform, walking in half circles round the tree. The way he walks – slight tilt of the head, a deliberate swing in the arms, measured step – I know he has become excited with some idea. He looks at me and then looks away, saying nothing. He is taking his time.

'In times like these, those who don't take a stand – politically, I mean – must be shot,' he blurts out at last and pushes his glasses further up the bridge of his nose. I say nothing. Perhaps he, too, does not expect a response, for he is walking on the platform, much in the same way as before, without looking at me. Is he talking to himself? All the same this is an opportunity to broach a subject I have avoided previously. So I say: 'A bit harsh, no?'

'Oh, you find it harsh? Really?' I have misjudged him. He wants the conversation as much as I do, a tiring affair, but little can now be done about it. 'On the other side of these forests,' he continues, 'why, at their very centre, at various places along the river, people are suffering. Countless homes flooded, countless displaced. Why? Because we want only wastelands! And what is better, we're all for progress. Some *progress* this! Now ask yourself who pays the price for this progress? Not you and me, for sure. Not yet. Genuine people's movements to save their homes, to protect themselves are crushed or ridiculed as propaganda. Big money changes hands. Voices are stifled, and there are many ways to do that. And amid all this we happily go about our business. And what business! The practice of law! Something we don't give a damn about. Thankfully, I may be only accused of this.' He has fallen silent, no, he is anticipating my question and preparing a response. Already the talk is turning into a game. A mere battle of wits. Will it ever rise above that?

'And what else is to be my blame?' I humour him.

'You're a writer, too, and you care about that.' Finally he is looking at me. 'Yet all you want to write about is Proust and Mendelssohn, Paris and chess. Books plotted like games. Stories with musical variations. Esoteric, surely. Imaginative and timeless and dead.'

'That and more,' I reply. 'Melancholy, for instance.' I cannot think of much else. He has summarized it well.

'Yes, what about it?' he asks.

'Nothing at all, now that I think. But then people write for several reasons. For instance, you may find language a living thing, throbbing with life. You may like fondling it, squeezing it even. That may become your only concern. Or you may busy yourself in forming a world superior to this one, even as it borrows, here and there, a gesture, a glance, a mote of dust, the colour of sky – a world that hasn't vanished the next moment because the growing randomness has thrown everything into disarray.'

'Yes, yes, metaphors, exercises in style. Imagination surmounting reality. Isn't that what you say? But I tell you, that rarefied air you breathe rises from this very ground. For what, after all, makes a thing imaginary or real? I've seen children displaced from their homes, walking in the dark, frail and hungry and fearful – there's nothing *real* in their faces.'

'We reach the absurd through different ways,' I say resignedly.

At this he nods. He understands what I mean. We are silent now. A cow is grazing on tufts of wild grass on the other side of the hedge, a bell tinkling with each movement of its head. The clouds have flown away leaving a streak of white in the sky. The heat is rising. My friend asks me if we should return to the room.

Inside, I quickly slip through the mosquito net and lie down on my back, my arms crossed under my head. My friend not without some difficulty has taken his favourite place on the mantlepiece, the area behind his legs a garish pink in colour, the hearth clean and awaiting winter. He has put on weight. To me, though, he often says that I remain thin as a snake. Comfortably settled, he resumes the talk from his vantage point: 'All those movements in art that emerged from the war – be it Dadaism, Surrealism or the Nouveaux Réalistes – were a protest against something, no? Against the bourgeois sensibilities and imperialist interests that had made art opaque and insensitive to the suffering of people. You take that essence out of those movements – what in fact ultimately happened – and all you're left with is chaos.'

The thought comes to me that his language is becoming all too familiar.

'Yes, chaos,' I murmur. 'The curse of expecting art to do things it isn't meant to do. Today, it's become the province of mostly those who should be the farthest from it.'

'What can it not do?'

'For instance, poems written and recited in binary codes. At a reading to which I persuaded myself to go out of sheer boredom. Now how does that express the suffering of people?'

'That is shit. It expresses nothing.'

'And how does a landscape express this suffering?'

'I don't know.'

'So should we do away with landscapes altogether?'

'You cunning bastard.'

'Maybe with any luck,' I say, 'we may have what you call a "civilized society" in another thousand years. Let's assume there'll be little or no suffering of the kind you speak. Yet other forms of suffering will survive. I'm simply doing my bit to keep that part alive. Good luck to others who're doing the rest.'

'You cunning bastard.' Laughter is forming in his throat. It rises and rises until it issues forth from his lips and spreads across the room and escapes through the chimney. I am smiling too. All is square between us once more.

'Tell me about the book you were speaking of the other day. That novel by Bioy Casares,' he says suddenly. I ask him if he would rather not read it himself. If I reveal the ingenious plot what will remain! 'No, go ahead. Who knows when I'll get a chance.'

He is still perched on the mantle when I finish. He releases a low whistle. It has taken me little over four minutes to tell the story. He admits he has never heard something like it. 'Now, there you've a book that'll survive a thousand years,' he says at last, whether in earnest or not, I cannot tell. A knock, and the caretaker enters, which can only mean that lunch is ready. It is only quarter past noon. This place is full of time, it never seems to run out. How will I learn again to live in a city where time is as nimble as a cat.

Later, after the meal, we saunter through the gallery towards our room. At the bend, we stand and observe the church spire that rises above the trees in the distance. 'We should look it up before we leave tomorrow,' I say to him.

I am the first to wake up. It is only half past three in the afternoon. My friend is lightly snoring. A bee slips through the ventilator, hovers above the fan, then takes a sudden dip with a buzzing sound and hits the floor. There it crawls, striving not to forget that skill, rises again and settles in some crevice where it finally falls quiet. I have been reading for an hour when he stirs and asks, as if talking in his sleep, if we can go to the waterfall. The heat has passed and the wind has picked up again. We take turns in the shower and in about forty minutes are walking on the road that skirts the meadows before it bends to the right to leave behind this town for faraway places. About a hundred yards from the bend eucalyptuses, standing in a series of hemicycles converging into one another, do their best to obstruct the view of the governor's cottage. Somewhere near is the mud-trail that cuts through the forest and descends into the depths. A tin board affixed to the trunk of a pine points in the direction of the trail: it is two miles to the falls.

Hills seem to get taller and taller as we approach the falls. The leaves of trees that grow in these shadowy parts are of a pale green silhouetted against a sky, blue and full of light, where a half moon is already beginning to show. The trees are unusually silent, there are no birds or animals visible to the eye. My friend finds a second trail that saves us some walking and I am tempted to try. Halfway, we slip over dry leaves and it is only a miracle that we manage to come up on both legs on the other side. My sight falls on a kitten tearing apart a mouse in a cleft along the trail. We continue to walk, and soon we begin to hear the plash of water. Crossing a wooden bridge, which looks as if it will not see another summer, we go down a few steps cut into the hill, and find ourselves standing at the edge of the pool into which water is falling in narrow streams over the rocks on the other side: this is all that remains of the waterfall. We wash our faces and, removing our shoes, dip our legs in the pool. Its coolness makes us light and cheerful. Two boys emerge from under the waterfall, their brown skins glisten as they run naked towards the brush where they have left their clothes. Taking turns rubbing each other with a rag brought for that purpose, they talk in a language we cannot understand.

My friend is now telling me about his trip into the interiors with a tribal leader during his election campaign last winter: 'Thick clouds had covered the moon. But on either side of the road, sleeping in the open, were countless people who had walked long distances through the forest to see their leader. People caught in the war between the government and the guerrillas. Uprooted and fearing for their lives. The guerrillas in the forests prodded them every now and then to join in *their* war, while the state was doing all it could to make them soldiers in a very special kind of 'civil resistance' – note the irony – by promising each of them a self-loading rifle and a paltry allowance. Moving them to camps set up for this purpose alone. Forcibly removing people from their homes and disrupting their peaceful existence to help the state fight the guerrillas. And when they tired of all this fighting they could always be useful to the industries in the region. What a scheme! Isn't it incredible? And we still have a real beauty of that book with all the world's protections against abuse of civil liberties.

'A snake. A long, red snake melting into the horizon. That's how I first saw all those people patiently walking to the assembly, to listen to their leader, to pledge support. I felt there was some point in all this.' My friend has fallen silent, the way he does when he is confused or simply unwilling to waste more words.

I know what happened. I have heard it before. I have felt it before. You can taste the success on your lips, but it is only a word spiralling in your head. It never comes. Something else comes in its place. Failure. Disappointment. I do not say any of this to him. Instead I tell him we are, in our separate ways, in the lonely business of rolling dice and dealing cards. We may learn tricks on the way, but that is about all we can do.

It is getting dark and we have a long climb ahead. By the time we cross the battered bridge, the light has left the sky; it is weightless, rising higher and higher until stars puncture its fabric. In a hut, just where the climb begins, a solitary man has kindled a fire and is playing a flute. Gloom fills my heart and mercifully ejects all fears of the dark, of animals and phantoms. But my friend walks fast, and every now and then lights a match, perhaps to scare away creatures hiding in the trees or in the rocks. Breeze that is by turn cool and warm flows over us, taking away the drops of sweat on our faces and necks. We stop only twice to get our wind back. We reach the road in less than a quarter of an hour. My fingers are swollen, I move them like apes do to make them thin and long again.

My friend has to make a call, and I need a sip of water. So we walk along the road that cuts across the meadows to the kiosk where we take turns drinking from a bottle before he goes into one of the phone booths. I want to call her. But I know there is little point; the pit of despair separates us. A beating of drums lures me out of the kiosk. I find locals arrive in small groups and assemble in a nearby ground where a strange rite has commenced – men and women, joined to one another in chain-like formations, perform some sort of a tap dance around an effigy, their feet churning dust to the beat of the drums. I grab a boy from the shoulder and ask about the ceremony. From whatever little I gather it is to commemorate the recent death of one of their kin. To me it sounds nothing like the music of grief, and maybe it is not. I do not realise when my friend joins me. We watch until clouds of dust have completely filled the ground and only the beating of drums can be heard.

For dinner we eat a local form of spaghetti cooked in a red sauce. Before I fall asleep, just as I close my eyes, I see the words 'SHOOT TO KILL' painted in white on the cliff that towers above the shooting range inside the cantonment.

Next morning we walk towards the church under a sky low and grey with clouds. There are pines around it, but the grounds look pale and unkept. Under a few trees, stone benches gather dust, awaiting visitors. The church is over a century old though it appears much older, like a medieval chapel in some Scottish village. It is open now, and you can see people sitting in the pews listening to the vicar who is making most of this opportunity, reciting in an animated voice and a language I can barely understand something to do with a tussle between Christ and Lucifer. Outside, several shoes and slippers are stacked in pairs next to the front wall: harmless temple practices brought over to other doorsills. While my friend busies himself with observing the stonework, I drift towards a bench where a little girl is sitting, absorbed in a game of marbles she is playing with herself. The sound of my approaching step makes her look up. Her small arms and legs are coated with dust, her hair unwashed and her frock dirty and torn in places; the skin of her face is parched and scabrous. Yet her eyes are alive, deep dark pools that will drown anything that falls into them. And with these liquid eyes, she smiles at me, and the smile enters me, fills me.

Tahiti

One who loves must share the fate of his loved one.
Mikhail Bulgakov

I

For some time now I have lived in the hills, in a settlement built a century or two past with not a few old, impressive structures in it. What will, what labour must have gone into them, today less than a drop in the pool of time. Weight of age-old stone on trembling spines, again and again and again. Occasionally, they'd bring to mind an ancient monastery I had visited in those remote mountains of which Kipling had spoken so reverentially, towering high atop a cliff, blunting its summit. Above was the clear blue sky and behind the rugged precipices, snow in their highest crevices, even as the dry terrain below merged far off into the horizon.

That thrust which begat art in rocks so close to heavens is lost on us. Maybe some of it remains. There still exist a few who deliver up to its call, perishing gladly drinking its glory. But enough of this. Why obscure a plain matter unnecessarily?

The place I speak of is spread over two adjoining hills. Twenty-one even-sized cottages with slanting tile roofs mark the

47

green slope of one hill in a rising curve. Together, they give the impression of a large orange boomerang lying on the grass as the road suddenly bends about the hill across the valley, clearing the view. Most of the cottages are privately owned, the few remaining ones have been retained by the authorities for lodging senior public servants on a holiday. Pines and deodars climb the hills from all sides creating a most picturesque landscape. At its centre is a clubhouse, circular in shape with an aquamarine dome, that provides for satellite television and indoor recreation, houses a small pool and a bar serving some very fine spirits.

To reach the cottages you must first negotiate the winding road about the neighbouring hill that in its lower stretch is arrested on either side by shops of everyday supplies and local craft dealers such as are common in small mountain towns, and a few eating places. Upon climbing up from the bazaar for about half a mile the road suddenly forks, one half dropping slightly to the left meanders about the hill, crosses over to the next, and ends at the clubhouse, while the other half continues its ascent amid ancient pines to reach a clearing where an old library and the ruins of a church keep each other company. Visitors are not many and chiefly consist of friends or families of those who own the cottages. Locals are scattered in the lower folds of the hills living mostly in a dismal state.

Like the cottages, the clubhouse is a colonial legacy. It is managed and maintained by means of a yearly grant from the authorities and an annual fee paid by its members. Most of the cottages are vacant all the time; their owners come visiting once in a few years when the psychosis of living seeps so deep that they are obliged to take the air.

On my first visit to the clubhouse the manager gladly took me around and offered me drinks. Being new to the place, I was somewhat surprised at being so entertained. But later it occurred to me that the settlement's obscurity had snuffed out any opportunities that could have been available to the locals to earn a trifle extra. Barely receiving a few guests in a year limited his secondary earnings considerably and, smelling an opportunity, he entertained me for two full hours.

Outside it had become incredibly dark. Black clouds with bloated bellies had crept from the north, swallowing up the stars. He said it would snow in the night, and I saw this as my chance. I paid, adding a handsome tip. It appeared to me that I would need his company one way or the other as time moved on.

Seasons change. Nights assault days more easily with the approaching winter. It snowed on my first night up here. All night I watched the snow fall while Bach played in the background, lost in a kind of tug-of-war between the past and the future.

But today? Today nothing. Nothing except this silence, this wish for the world to come anew simply through my being.

I arrived here seven months ago. At about noon one day I found myself negotiating the bend about the hill I described before. A two-hour ride in an old and rickety bus from the town where I had been staying for a week. In the early hours of that morning there were not many passengers in the terminal. I sat some rows behind the driver and looked out to the several stalls with tin roofs which served tea and snacks to passengers and crowded either side of the terminal's entrance. To begin with it had not been a bright morning, but as I took the seat on the bus the clouds quickly thickened and soon there was snow.

The attendant at the rest house where I had stayed for a week had told me about the settlement. He described it, as hill men do, with such vividness that I was interested. He offered to make arrangements for my stay there – he knew of a cottage that was available on rent. From there on things fell smoothly in place.

Trumpeting through the outskirts of town, the bus joined the sparse traffic on the route to the settlement. The road, cut into the mountainside, passed through a wooded expanse and not infrequently looked upon the valley that was progressively being covered with a thin coat of snow. From my window I saw how the snowflakes fell silently on the pine needles and, unable to maintain their hold, slipped down to the ground. The pines looked like giants standing up in snow with bated breath watching the bus move at its leisurely pace. A profound silence hung over the entire forest. The only sound you heard clearly was of the overworked engine that seemed to suggest a lifetime of service, now in need of an overhaul. There were hardly a few passengers in the bus. The one sitting across had already dozed off with his legs closed tightly around a large dirty sack of potatoes. Two rows behind sat a woman with a young girl; the girl, wrapped in woollens, now and then mumbled something in the woman's ear that did not fail to bring a smile to the her lips.

In that white morning, for a reason I could scarcely fathom, I felt the darkness lift slightly. I recalled how, for far too long a time, I had wandered through life like a sleepwalker, walking through streets barely familiar. The city had oppressed me much and at last I was happy to escape from it. For some years, I had been attached to a publishing firm, a job that I had held on to since my early runaway success as a writer.

Then on one of those days when you can see it clearly for all its worth, I resigned from the firm and, upon completing a few pending assignments, found myself heading for the mountains.

Ah, the mountains. They rise before you from the depths of earth and in no time reach the blue dome, where – near their crown – they too take on a bluish hue.

II

The weather cleared up just as the bus crawled through the narrow street of the bazaar. Leaving the bus I found a tea stall where men were drinking tea and chatting incessantly. I sat on a bench and waited. In the distance, I could see the conical roof of the abandoned church that had somehow managed to escape the pine cover closing on it. Also visible slightly below, as I was soon to find out, was the cupola of the building that housed the library.

Sitting beside me was the man who had slept during the entire journey with his legs tightly closed round the sack of potatoes, sipping tea and absorbed in thought. He did not notice me at first, but then recovering somewhat asked if I was a first-time visitor. He smiled easily, a smile that deepened the creases on his face and left bare a tale of hardships, slight melancholy clouding his eyes. I asked him for directions to the cottages, which he clearly provided. Then balancing the sack across his back, he swiftly descended into the valley by the steep mud path that lay behind the stall.

At first I strolled through the bazaar looking now and then at the displayed items outside the shops. But before long the road was climbing into the mountain. In half an hour, I was at the fork, from where I looked back to take in the scene – shades of green with snow here and there, light clouds settling over the valley and the sun glowing feebly in the cobalt sky – which, then, seemed to me the summation of all beauty.

I soon reached the cottages. Something in the symmetry of the place made all of it look atemporally removed from the modern world, to its anxieties and its distrust in the destiny that binds all. I was in time for lunch, but first I was taken around the house – empty for its owner lived abroad.

My room was to the left of the main sitting area that opened on to a verandah where, in a corner, there was an easy chair and near its foot a low table, both made of walnut wood. It was warm and comfortable with a medium-sized bed and side cabinets perched on one of which was an anglepoise lamp. Under the window, through which a tall deodar could be seen, was a writing desk with a cane chair. There was a music player too. The room had a fireplace; on its mantlepiece was an attractive glass bottle holding a yacht in its belly. The yacht was made of different coloured crystals. The glass restricted human contact as if human touch was the deadener, human touch robbing things of their value.

After lunch I settled in the easy chair with the Mallarmé. But I did not begin instantly. Instead I watched the valley receive, like a vast bowl, the slanting rays of the sun. I was tempted to close my eyes a moment, and then, all at once, I saw Asya.

Driving past the fields that turned the countryside yellow. The road smooth and clear, a local radio station playing popular music. Then a small lake formed by the backwaters of a dam. The sun making the water flash silver. Mustard crops beyond the lake. A solitary cloud lingering near the sun. My kiss on her nape, my face in her hair.

III

At eight in the evening, the late August sun was growing pale, and the Seine shimmered in its last light. I had spent most of the day wandering about Montmartre visiting antiquarian shops and kiosks where one may purchase a Van Gogh or Gauguin for a trifle, and had towards late afternoon settled at a restaurant on Rue de Rivoli, not far from Notre Dame, reading an essay by that blind old Argentine whose works combine the fantastic with the commonplace, distil metaphysics into magic.

Now my eyes were locked on its coarse blue cover. Out of nothing, a bizarre yet remotely familiar thought had acquired weight: wasn't the book as much alive as the reader, the words and characters inside continuously arranging and rearranging themselves to suggest a myriad of stories, constructs, universes.

At half past six I found myself near Invalides, from where I resumed my journey on foot, without much cause, along Quai d'Orsay towards the Eiffel Tower. Walking beneath the line of maples, the Seine by my side, I fell prey to a sudden bout of sadness, and knew not how to escape it. 'A cruise on the Seine.' In all these days I hadn't once thought of the river, but now it seemed the only reasonable thing to do.

Waves lashing against stone. How I loved that sound, now coming to me all mixed up with the noise of the evening traffic on Quai d'Orsay. My pace had slowed down, and soon I fell under the spell of random thoughts.

I imagined us in a garden, walking along a path that cut through a flower bed beyond which lay a carpet of green, lush under a bright sun. The path dipped so very slightly and in time exposed a split – in the distance could be seen a baroque palace on whose white walls towering palms, standing like minarets in four corners, left interesting shadows as the rays broke over them. The branching paths met again at the palace gates.

At the fork, then, we parted. But why? That first step was the wrong step. In a moment everything vanished, and the palace hovered like a flame on the edge of vision. Only the path remained; unchanged, testing, as each walked for days, for months, for years, never meeting the other. Yet the desire did not extinguish even as the body perished and the soul melted away in its own nothingness.

Now we were at the fork again, and a fine rain was falling. It fell all the while we walked through disparate landscape, through water, air and ether, fell for an immeasurably long time. At last we entered the palace, time or rain seemed to have changed little. But what was this? Why did she look at me as if seeing me for the first time? Her eyes were lifeless like a mirror, reflecting all that fell to their lot. Eyes that had become a mirror, not of within but of without.

And yet I stood right there looking at her. She came a step closer and held me in her arms. Something remarkable happened then: in an instant we were inside the palace gates, amid the palms, the lawns, the flowers, the fountains. Off its courtyard, we found a room, empty except a huge triangular bed in a corner. Large mirrors on opposite walls expectantly waited to endlessly multiply the one image.

A careless nudge of a jogger broke my reverie, dissolving the last tremors of dream. What took form was the lustrous water of the Seine, the din of automobiles, lovers delighting in each other, the Tower – Paris.

It is then that I notice her, sitting on a bench, held captive by a book with a black leather binding. She appears to be enjoying herself, for a smile is collecting at the corners of her mouth. Her face, mysteriously elegant, is remotely familiar too, smooth forehead, hair straight and lustrous that curls very slightly near the shoulders. My stare disturbs her, and she moves her attention away from the book, directs it at me. Now her sight rests on me (or pierces through me?) for a moment or two, but then, dismissing me, promptly returns to the script. It is enough, this slight gesture on her part, revealing to me those clear brown eyes that mock me faintly.

Waiting in the queue for the ferry, I see her again, at the other end, enjoying the evening breeze. She is alone, unperturbed. At times, she looks away to gaze at the Tower that deflects the sun's rays.

I found a seat in the penultimate row where the glass cover did not obstruct the view and observed how the wind and the dying sun had made the scene painting-like. About me, people moved chaotically to find seats of their choice.

Next to me is an unoccupied seat. Just then she walks into the ferry and comes up to me and inquires if I am holding it for someone. When I decline, she smiles and sits beside me. This is the time the dream has me in its clutch. She is saying something to me but I don't hear or can't hear. She is already inside me, she is me. Her face is my face too. How incredible! I can hear myself. And here, in Paris, of all places! I see the book in her lap. It is a Mallarmé. Oh, now she is telling her name. What was that? Tahiti? It depends, she says. It changes from one season to the next, from place to place, like names always do or appear to. But,

I resist, that's an island in the Pacific. That is how she is is all she offers. Yes, I think, you are an island drifting in a sea of countless, unknowable faces.

IV

Sitting beside her, consuming her presence, allows me hope. It drowns me in a sudden, vague happiness. She is listening to the voice from the handset that is describing the history of the palaces, the bridges, the museums that watch over the Seine. Light is fast fading from the air, letting in the darkness. The ferry's slow pace, the darkening of the sky, the softly glowing façades, and her sweet, spicy smell, together work as a calmative. Now she is telling me that the tempo of the commentator's voice is harmonious with the boat's speed (in what all can women see harmony!). It gives the impression, she says, of someone whispering in your ear, someone here, next to you, watching the world as if through your own eyes but understanding its enigmas better.

For a moment, I look at her closely. Then I search for the handset which is dangling beside my seat. Pulling it by its metallic coil, I hold it to my ear. She strains a bit to control her laughter. Where *are* you? What are you thinking? First, I say nothing. But later, like a fool, I let her in. I tell her that she makes me happy.

I do? That's all there is to it. A doubt, a pose. No, there's more: It's the evening, she says. Serene yet mischievous. Full of surprises, revelations. On evenings like these wishes come true.

I still held the handset to my ear. The voice coming from it was speaking of gargoyles, that they are nothing but sculpted gutters acting as spouts to carry water clear of a wall. Scores of them jutted out of the walls of Notre Dame, its edges, and its spire. The lady in front of me hurriedly clicked pictures before it or whatever was left of it vanished into the darkness.

The ferry took a turn about the cathedral, circumscribing Ile de la Cité. Wasn't that Hugo peeping from behind a gargoyle? Because of Notre Dame, of course. Hugo, and not Proust. Proust could never have been up there. His image was of a ghost lying in bed, half-covered by a blanket, writing in the light of a lamp, and hemmed in by those cork-lined walls, silently sinking to death in the web of his own memories or what he was trying to make of them. It was too prodigious an impression to overcome: to interrupt his undertaking seemed a disservice to literature I could ill afford. I settled with Hugo.

The ferry has just crossed Pont Neuf on its way back when she speaks again. This time she probes the past: Where is she? I don't know, so I shake my head.

She is looking at me, but her gaze is soft and there is just a flicker of irony in it. Her lips are now nearly touching my ear. She's made a suggestion. A place where we can go dancing. In fact there are two. A close friend, she confides, plays at a nightclub in Montmartre – Odéon it's called – and sometimes at a bohemian jazz bar, too, in St-Germain-des-Prés. Tomorrow, at eight.

The Tower was sparkling with a colourful display of lights. My dream was nearing its end; come to think of it, it couldn't go much longer. Soon, I reasoned to myself, the ferry will hit the dock, passengers will disembark one after the other, and so will she. No, I thought, not yet.

Tomorrow, certainly. But what now? I'd like you to stay a bit longer. I am almost ashamed of myself. Little control over my tongue off which words bounce forth impetuously. She says she has to meet somebody. A friend who once bailed her out of a fix. She doesn't need to say more. But she does: You'd agree that friendships formed in adventure, tragedy, or misdeed are closer to heart than those cemented by affection or respect. Darkness is more beautiful than the light, is it not? So full of intrigue and infidelities. Besides, he leaves for Egypt tomorrow and proposes never to return.

Ah, the poet she is turning out to be! What can I say to hold her back? Already I see them drinking and eating, discussing their past that somehow binds them intimately. I see her in his arms, their bodies close as they dance to soft music. What is this? Jealousy? Perhaps she has seen it too, for she speaks from under the shade of empathy: We can meet early tomorrow if you aren't busy. We can roam around and then later we can go to the club.

Although I plan to visit the library at Sorbonne the next day, I keep this to myself. She is fast learning the game, offering me a continuum. I just have to pretend that her evening away is a part of the dream, and in no time she will be with me once more. We are the last to disembark, walking close to one another. On climbing the stairs that join the pier to Pont d'Iéna, standing beneath the shining Tower, the shaft of light at its crown rotating above the darkened city like the outstretched limb of a compass, she suggests we meet at the Boulevard Saint-Michel, near the entrance of the Luxembourg.

That is close to where I stay, I reply for the sake of it.

So much the better. You won't be late then. See you at noon!

O you poor bastard, full of expectancy and loneliness, what an engaging phantom you had crafted to lighten your burden.

Once she had left, I started walking towards the train station. Not far from the station I saw an Italian bistro and thought of having something to eat. I found a table next to a window from where you could watch the trains cross the Seine every once in a while. There, waiting for my order, I reconstructed, little by little, the day that had not been uneventful.

V

Of the time I speak, the city was not as one sees it today. Like any other old city, it was a metropolis of reserve and character. Modern capital had not yet punctured its melancholy; life was more or less peaceful and without pretence. Under the veil of political and bureaucratic torpor, there was a certain playfulness in its spirit.

Winter was coming, that time of the year which always made the sky clear and blue. With a hint of chill in the noon wind, the sun's warmth gave comfort. We had been to the cinema, and were now sitting on a bench beside an ice-cream parlour digging our spoons in a sundae. Close to the bench was a fig tree from where a myna whistled to us from time to time. Asya had been uncommonly reticent, and I had asked her about it a few times. She had denied this, yet I knew there was something to it. Nothing though that I couldn't have dispelled as pointless.

But how wrong you are, how foolish. How you think light and bliss will last forever when the void is opening at your feet. And to fall into it is your only destiny. Oh, but why deviate? Come forth without further circumlocutions, and speak of how when night fell over that day and anytime thereafter you have known little peace. Tell how when you saw the void only too late you felt vertigo from which you could never recover. Like a ghost you wandered, consuming days aimlessly with a wish to reach the end of time and see beyond, to embrace it and at long last begin anew.

Her house wasn't far away and we began walking towards it. She lived in one of those pretty places in the south of the city, close to the institute of technology, where it is so enjoyable to walk in the evenings. She was talking to me, but I was lost in strange images of the days ahead. Lamps that lit up the street threw faint shadows on the ground, a sickle of a moon was slowly climbing up in the sky. Suddenly there swelled in me an irresistible urge to embrace her, to make one final effort. First I held myself back, but then, unable to hold my reserve, I put my arms around her. She did not resist, but her body felt slightly stiff. I wasn't discouraged: where the bond is strong, discouragement doesn't come easily. I moved to kiss her, but she bent her head a little and my lips ended up brushing her cheek. Tears welled up in my eyes and, turning away without a word, I walked into the growing darkness.

I did not see her again. But my mind, rather obstinately, kept reliving the past – a past which had already started to look obscure and meaningless. A past you have to fight, a duel from which you don't emerge free of scars.

In time time went astray. I couldn't keep up with it. Days melted into each other, and I went tumbling through them, all along thinking of those eyes that had been so still they reflected whatever fell to their lot: those clear brown eyes had been a mirror not of within but of without.

Having spent a month or so in this timelessness, I decided a change of place might do me good. I called up my sister in London, where she taught at a city college, and on a damp December morning left the city.

VI

Whereas it had snowed in the night, a bright morning sun was shining above the mountains, stoking the air with light. Snow that had collected on the ground and in solemn nooks was starting to melt under its warmth. Misty vapours rose from it and quickly vanished into the brightness. Although I had watched the snow fall all night, I was not tired. The evening before, having drained away the weariness in the shower, I had gone to the clubhouse.

When I left the bar at about ten it was dark and cold outside, and I wasted little time to get to my room. It was comfortably warm, with the electric heater in the hearth doing the job well. I decided to play *Goldberg Variations*. In a while, it began to snow.

Next morning I thought of exploring the place. The previous day, walking through the bazaar, I had seen the spire of a church, and to its side the cupola of a building which had appeared round and big. I asked the caretaker about it. He told me that it was an old library, perhaps the oldest in this part of the country. It felt like a piece of luck, and seeing that I was interested he handed me a few more details. Thus I came to know that the library had some very rare books and first editions, and that it was more or less neglected by the authorities and would have fallen into disuse had it not been for the librarian, a foreigner, old and solitary, half blind, who continued to petition for and receive a yearly grant to run it. He informed me that the old man (they had never learnt how to pronounce his name, and now nobody remembered it) had no family and no one could tell exactly why and how he had come here of all places. He rarely left the library these days, but twice a week gave lessons to a few children from nearby villages. Aside from these children, he said to me, people up here have forgotten the old man and the library.

By then my mind was made up. A library hidden in the mountains seemed a little misplaced. It appeared as if, upset with the world, it had chosen its exile and with a half-blind old man for a guardian created for itself a peaceful oblivion.

At about noon I walked to the library. Amid the pines it was fairly cold, but the climb warmed me up a little. Here and there light broke through the green cover and birds chirped in chorus. The path went rising and falling and curving into the mountain. Then all at once the vista opened and I saw the abandoned church that in the silence appeared majestic; icicles that hung from its eaves were slowly melting away. To my left was the library which, together with the old church stood at the edge of a precipice that gave away into a deep narrow valley from where came the faint gurgling sound of a stream.

One of the large heavy doors was partly open and I slipped in. I came into some sort of a hallway. Here it was bright and warm, but the air had a whiff of that distinct smell which is produced by the slow decaying of paper. Beneath a large circular dome there were wide glass ventilators through which the outside light came into the building. From the centre-space beneath the dome tall open cabinets stretched out in every direction. Even-sized metal plates affixed at the top of each cabinet indicated the different categories: 'PURE SCIENCES', 'LITERATURE', 'PHILOSOPHY', so on and so forth. To my left was a large librarian's desk that nearly concealed a wide cabinet made of pigeonholes. It was entirely free of cards. The whole place seemed to have turned inwards.

At first I saw no one, for the man who was quietly working in a corner under a feeble lamp was so small that it was not difficult to miss him in the vast surroundings. Merrily enjoying his work, he had not seen me. I felt a little apologetic to disturb him, but I called at last. My words had no effect on him. I called again. This time he raised his head and looked at me. I saw that his face was in proportion to his body, small and thin with a reddish complexion, a beak of a nose, and tiny eyes as if made of glass like a sparrow's. His head nearly free of hair was kept warm by a woollen balaclava rolled up to just about his ears. His eyes had in them a somewhat searching look and at the same time a certain inner quiet.

About him were two stacks of paper. One blank and another covered with minute well-formed letters in purple ink, written in a delicate hand. A red hardbound book lay next to the stack of blank pages. Its spine told me it was a Carlyle – *Sartor Resartus*. I wanted to say something – anything – when, recovering from his thoughts, he asked in his faint and very slightly accented voice what I thought of his library.

At last I managed to say something. He seemed to weigh my words in his mind. Then his eyes appeared confident and he offered me a chair. I sat down and for a moment watched how the sun's rays fell on some of those books, accentuating the slow process of their decay.

We spoke of libraries. The power they possess, the lure to lose oneself in them. Now his eyes were glowing – what can be of more interest to one who has given his life to books?

Are you a poet, sir? Not quite, I replied. Only a writer. This seem to pique his interest and he asked about my books. What could I say? I haven't written a book in years, I finally revealed to him, and the few slim titles I wrote years ago dropped like stones in water. But in the first place, I was sort of expecting this. In a way, the book that will define me lies unwritten.

He said he would make his own judgement if I could show him one of my novels. I didn't have any with me, but told him I would arrange one for him in due course. Then, not knowing why, I said something stupid: These books are quite old. What would you guess their age to be?

They're old, yes, aren't they? Most of them are from the fifties or before. If I recall well, no book has entered the library in a decade. The grant is barely enough to pay for maintenance.

His words made me look. Maybe it was the way he spoke, as if he could very nearly see the end of one of those books. Countless unread stories awaited me to set them free of the very words that held them captive. If only I would read them and allow them refuge in my head where, free of a form or structure, they could float at leisure. I was tempted to liberate them, to read them, one after the other, till I had set the very last one free. How ephemeral, I thought, is the process of creation, of writing books, of lending random words to equally random thoughts merely to grant another the privilege of release.

The voice of the old man broke into my thoughts: But there's little sense in preserving these books for posterity. I tell you, the day they lose their perishable nature they will cease to interest us. Only through their mortality do they live in us.

I instantly thought of the Web – which is nowhere and every-where, a well of immortality. As if he could read my thoughts, as if we were already at a level where words were useless, he added: I'm told in cities these days there're invisible libraries where everything is stored in dockets that don't grow old, aren't destroyed by the excesses of time or water, heat or cold, that exist yet not exist at the same time. Of course, there isn't a need of such a system up here. An old friend who is a librarian at a city college came visiting last year. Unlike previous times, he said, the boundaries of information have now become porous, that a new age had dawned, an age where one could go anywhere with a click of a button.

He was now looking into the distance where broad beams of light were pouring through the glass ventilators. Believe me, he spoke again, all this speed, this information is our curse. We suffer from it and in the end will die of it.

Later he told me how in the night when his sight failed him he could locate a book simply by directing his thoughts to it. With him I saw, as time moved on, what I had always known – that books cast a spell too. The last bit of magic left to us.

I asked him if I could look around. He nodded his small head and, dismissing me, promptly returned to his task of smothering sheets with slim purple letters that he formed with great attention and a little stress.

Leaving him to his work, I went past tall cabinets looking for a book that may have interested me. In one place I found an old book by Novalis and began to leaf through its pages that were beginning to come apart from the spine, uttering aloud a phrase now and then. The man's voice filled the silence: Novalis. Good choice. Not even a ghost has touched it in years.

I turned round and saw that he hadn't moved from his place. What was more, he hadn't even raised his head and was absorbed as before. But how then could he tell? I know them, my books, very well, his voice came from somewhere far away. I haven't spent these last many years for nothing. I can even tell them from the sound they make.

It left no doubt that he still possessed a sharp ear which allowed him his little amusement. I asked if I could borrow the book for a while.

We shook hands, and he asked me to come again. Then he spoke aloud the name I had given him. At that moment, for the first time in years, I was reminded of Tahiti, the Luxembourg Gardens. Strange thing memory is! De Quincey was right. Nothing goes away. All the ghosts dance around us in a circle. Forever and ever.

As I descended the hill, a dog began to follow me. Eyes with a sombre look in them, he was wasting away for lack of food. I had nothing to offer the poor beast, but I took him along. Reaching the fork, I went down towards the bazaar. I came to a tea-stall, big glass jars with tin lids lined its counter. Here I bought a pack of biscuits and fed the dog. He ate hurriedly, without rest. Three boys playing marbles nearby watched the spectacle with interest. Once full, the dog receded to a corner and closed his eyes. I had little inclination to walk down further and turned back to the cottages. No sooner had I begun than I found the dog yet again on my trail. However, by the time I reached the cottage, he had given me a slip.

With no desire to eat, I went straight to my room and stretched out on the bed. In no time, I had fallen into a deep sleep.

It was already evening. I asked for tea. Watching the vapours rise from the cup, a thought came to me. Somewhere in that thought was a way to begin again. How long has it been then? I rolled the word in my mouth.

I found some blank sheets, and settled down to write. Something. Anything. I was drawn back in time to that gloomy afternoon in London when I had written those first words. If I could only bring back some of that desire, that amazement.

The Novalis lay on the table. I stared at it awhile. Then I began. How else, if not with these mountains, and with this settlement so delicately sewn into them?

VII

Sleep came easily that night. Sleep carried me far off into a deep dark well where nothing could reach me. The past was one vast plain of sleep and dream, an immense steppe that would slowly come to cover everything.

All the same there remained the small matter of a meeting. Had the boat ride been for real? The image warmed a distant nerve somewhere.

The sun shining through the large windows was troubling me, with effort I helped myself out of bed and went into the balcony. I wasn't expected at the Luxembourg until noon, so I consumed the hours unhurriedly. I shaved, took a long slow shower, and ate a breakfast of toasts and cereals and coffee. Then I went out into the street. Soon I was walking along Boulevard de Port Royal where at that hour the traffic was light. It is, however, a task to keep the mind free of thoughts – thoughts of any kind. It requires an unswerving faith in the path given us. I had little of it to spare at the time. With each step a slow ache rose in me. For once, I even thought of abandoning the meeting and turning back, yet, unsure, I kept walking.

I see her now. She has the demeanour of a queen, dressed in a blue sleeveless blouse and an asymmetrical skirt that flutters about her legs. It doesn't take much from me to surrender. Thoughts evaporate and I begin to feel warm again. She has not seen me and is still looking away, towards the gardens. My voice startles her a little, just a little. She kisses me on the cheek. When she moves away, part of a café's striped awning is visible in the curve of her neck. This is how, I think, paintings are born.

We are in the park already. She is telling me something she read in the papers. But she cuts it off abruptly, it has just occurred to her that she doesn't know my name. No, don't tell me, she pleads, when I try to speak. We will find one for you. A new one. The old name won't do. There is mischief in her voice and a swing in her step. Alright, I say, and allow her time. She seems to turn a few names in her head before she settles on one. Because you write too, she tells me.

We found two empty chairs next to the pond, where not far from us some children played with their tiny yachts and paperboats. People lounged here and there, many walked leisurely round the palace enjoying the sun. Under a palm tree – so pleasing to the eye that it appeared artificial – a young couple kissed passionately. Birds cooed in the green lawns and amid the flowers that circled them.

I tell her about what I write. Crisp clean books. No philosophy, no moral in tow. About stars at dawn and wind through the pines, that sort of thing. Oh, I see now, she joins in. You're an artist. A real one. Always aloof. Not caring much about people. The world and its horrors. Well, nothing wrong in that.

But I do care about people, I object. I do care. That's why I write what I write.

How could I explain? I try anyway. I tell her that art has a precise function. To offer a glimpse of what it is *to be*. Every artist, every poet knows this and strives for this. All his attempts are to catch, if only fleetingly, a pure image, or even a shimmer of it. But, alas, this isn't an easy task – not by a long shot. Only art that is playful can begin to move towards this end, content that it is to simply flirt with life, not arrest it.

She appears to see my point. And anyway, she says, she was just joking. Her face though gives off a thoughtful look. A few very white clouds move unhurriedly across the sky. Then she asks if I will read to her one of my stories.

Later she tells me about the poetry she loves, about her life in Amsterdam, where she worked at a flower shop, where she read Rilke, Keats, Emily Dickinson, even Whitman, by the canal when the day was warm, where she grew enchanted with their verse and forgot to tend to business properly, where the lady who owned the shop was nice to her, where poetry was her sole indulgence, where she read on Sundays in her small attic-room, where she stretched on the bed and stared at the roof moving images in her head, where she prepared her dinner over an old stove and ate silently by herself, where she spoke aloud those lines to the night sky. Oh, how pleasant it was then.

She doesn't know why she came here. It seems a long time. An unexplained impulse. Or wait – why should she not tell – there was the dream. A vision perhaps. The night was cold and she had left the old stove burning to warm the room a little. Soon she was asleep. Then, all of a sudden, she heard a man's voice call her name. What was her name then? Didn't it begin with an E? Erica. Elinita. Anyway it isn't important. The voice roused her and she nearly jumped in bed, looking for its source. In the dim light of the stove, she saw a velvet curtain. It was slightly parted and behind it was some sort of an iron structure woven intricately with thick iron threads. From somewhere far off came the sound of moving water. The voice called again, distant this time, layered in the murmur of water. But now she understood it all. The Eiffel. The Seine. Paris, it seems, was beckoning her.

What a tale she wove. What a lament of longing. A voice imploring her to pass through a magic-curtain. From Amsterdam to Paris in three steps!

We both break into a sudden raucous laughter. Now I am certain I will never know what happened the night before. That man must already be on his way to Egypt. She is like a book in an unfamiliar script. I can love it, but I can't read it. Then, like a stab, the thought pierces me – why of all places was she sitting next to the river, so close to the Tower?

My musing was interrupted by a slight commotion nearby. One of the boys, going a little too far in his adventure, had fallen into the water head first, taking down his tiny yacht with him. He was quick to find his bearing and stand up. Standing waist deep in water assessing his loss, he cut a tragic figure. But the woman who I suppose was his mother did not share my sentiments. She pulled him out of the water and gave him a generous beating, which the boy received with what appeared to me a mix of stoicism and gratitude.

Love is a double-edged sword, she says to me. There's always a chance that you may cut yourself deeply.

VIII

We walked past the palace and then turned left from where, amid two lines of maples, the dome of the Panthéon entering the sky finished the picture quite agreeably. Crossing the Médicis Fountain, we came out into a narrow street. A light wind was blowing and the streets lay more or less deserted, buildings quiet, except some voices that erupted here and there from a shop or a tavern. People who passed us in the street looked at us with smiling eyes. A smell like that of ripe oranges wafted through the air and excited me. How perpetually surprising was the day with all its vicissitudes.

Exchanging one street for another we soon reached St-Germain-des-Prés. It was beaming with activity at that hour. Although the cobblestones pinched through my heelless moccasins, the air certainly had something encouraging about it. We went into a brasserie and ordered lunch. She ate with appetite, directing all her attention to the fare before her. This gave me the occasion to observe her. My mind drifted back to what she had told me. I recalled how on the previous day she sat reading Mallarmé next to the river, and how she had dismissed me without a thought. I had not held her interest for a moment then, passing through her eyes like all else that is routine passes through them, without stimulating the mind. Yet here I was, watching her, thinking about her, trying to forge a link between dream and reality.

She has caught me in my thoughts. To top it all, I have hardly eaten anything. She probes me. I tell her nothing is the matter.

Now I must swiftly recover. For she is still watching me, straw in her mouth, sipping her iced-tea. I order a café au lait. I slide back into the chair, rest my elbows on its lacquered arms, and coolly look around. A girl is sitting alone in a corner, dexterously punching the keys of her mobile phone, neglecting the cup before her.

I go back to her story. Surely, there's an image worth rescuing. I see her walk, arm in arm, with the man whose face I cannot see into the fading Parisian sun. And it is there, I think, I will begin my narrative, in the backwards: beginning with the two silhouettes growing dim in the distance as the sun once more leaves us in darkness to settle our abstruse, shadowy affairs.

But we are inexplicably open to oversimplify our desires. I was hopelessly unaware then of how the dice would roll. It rolled sooner than I had expected, and there I was – entering her story. Yet I did not write it for a long time, and when finally I did, she had become but a phantom floating through its pages, shrouded in mystery.

The silence is growing. I must do something. So I ask her about the plan for the evening. She gives it out in two words – the tango. The word fills me with dread. I can already feel my legs stiffen. Lewd dance of the slums.

Ah, the tango, I say finally. No need to say more. She has already sensed it. A smile is entering her face.

An old woman has seated herself on the adjoining table. She is observing us not without interest. Her hands rest on its edge, with the index and middle fingers of the right she drums rhythmically on the left closed into a fist. I smile at her and she smiles back.

We left the café and began to walk along Boulevard Saint-Germain. We talked, browsed books at second-hand dealers, discussed fashion as we walked past the mannequins put to display in store windows. Time seemed to gallop. Or was it not moving at all? It did not matter. Upon reaching the end of the boulevard, I offered to take her to Musée d'Orsay. But once near the museum we changed our minds. It was about six in the evening. The sun already appeared vague and decrepit, and a half moon was slowly forming in the sky. We found a bench close to the river. Then I told her a story I had written a few months ago. Slowly, the world, like a ball pushed into a dark corner, seemed to roll about us into the night.

A little after eight we reached the club in Montmartre. Her friend Amelio, the musician, had been informed beforehand. This Amelio, I was given to understand, could play many instruments, a virtuoso in the true sense of the word. Inside the lighting was dim, interspersed with thin red rays, as if made of fine dust, whose source you could not divine. At the time, there weren't many people in the club. Tables lay more or less vacant, and those present were all around the bar. Some were perched on stools, drinking and talking freely. Others stood in groups of two and three in dark corners. The air was still, but not stifling. Someone was playing a trombone. The notes emerged from the organ and moved sluggishly in a queue, the newer ones prodding the older ones, till they reached me. There was no sign of Amelio.

We found a table near the dais and ordered aperitifs. In the corner, close to the man playing the trombone an area had been kept clear of any furniture for the guests to dance in case the music broke their reserve. On the dais was a grand piano shrouded in semi darkness. A shadow moved over it. Then, just as the trombone-player was concluding his piece, the shadow joined in and a comping began. Before long the quirky cadences had immersed the entire place in a mad wave of delirium.

Post the performance, the trombone-player slipped past the curtains, leaving behind the shadow to entertain the audience. That shadow knew how to play. In no time the melancholy strains of the piano had drowned every other sound in the bar. It felt like a piece by Zez Confrey.

All this while people had been trickling into the nightclub, and the applause burst on us like a bomb. The shadow stepped back into the darkness. Now the place was overflowing with people. Voices more prominent than the soft waltz filtering through the speakers, bodies emitting sweet and musty smells by turn. The air was full with strains of music, jabber of people, clinking of glasses, and the smell of alcohol and sweat and perfumes.

A voice grows prominent with each word. The shadow at last gets a face, the colour of honey with deep dark eyes. Hands that could only belong to that face – those long knotted fingers, as good for the piano as for the chessmen.

Introductions follow spirits, spirits curl into smoke. We clink our glasses and the tiny air-globes shoot upwards. Amelio and Tahiti talk in whispers. Then she kisses me, takes his hand, and off they go to the dance floor. The music now has a quicker tempo and several people are dancing to its happy beats. Soon they are moving effortlessly with it, as if in a state of trance. Chutes of red light colour their faces. Even from a distance, I can see Amelio's shirt is nearly spoilt by sweat. Yet his cuffs are dry and sober, held fast by stone cuff links that sparkle with an orange flame. He is moving her about him like a child spinning a top with a sudden twist of his arm. And she moves like a tamed animal, with pleasure and abandon.

Later we talk and eat and drink. Amelio is telling us about his school days in the Andalusian mountains. He has read *Don Quixote* six times, but other picaresque novels of the Golden Age bore him silly. And in school he once acted in a play by Lope de Vega. His voice goes round and round like a blanket that keeps one warm on winter nights.

She has slid her arm into mine without a word. Suddenly, I can hear a staccato rhythm take over the music. A million pins enter through the soles of my feet and swiftly climb upwards. My head is swimming. She is holding me so close that I can feel the rise and fall of her chest. But – how can this be? – my feet are moving smoothly, in rhythm with her quick short steps. We must be in love to dance like this. Now she opens the embrace, now she closes in swiftly, flying off the ground.

When the beat ends, I kiss her on the nose. She kisses me back on the mouth. Bliss leaps in my heart, washes away the patina of pain. Off you go noble angel, I am done with your cold elegant wisdom!

Near midnight we come out into the street. Infinite universes spread their wings in the sky. So you heard me that night, I say to her. Of course, I did, she replies, tightening her hold on my arm. Eyes full of mischief. Eyes adept at hiding despair.

IX

Who says beauty is ephemeral, that it withers with the moment. Show me the person and I shall tell you he is a deceiver, a conjurer of falsity. For amid these elevations it is eternal, from sunup to sundown, from the first pine to the last star.

I now worked each day, some days more than others. Beginning with the present, I twisted time and made it circular, perhaps even arbitrary. Once more, I began shaping a world whose walls I built each day higher and higher, and into which I retired with sincere delight. Sometimes I saw a swallow alight on a branch of the deodar from where it sang to me its slow, sombre tunes. Each day the sun rose above the snows over the distant hills in the east, each night the moon hung in their cool shadow. I went along writing. Some days words easily slipped through my thoughts and took shape, on other days their indolence caused me great fatigue – I poked them here and there, and they turned and twisted without obliging. Till noon I worked in this way, seldom afterwards. Then I went out to explore the hills.

Before a month had passed, I had walked all the trails in all the mountains, I had discovered a tarn in the hills behind the settlement, I had stared at the heights. At other times, I would descend into a valley, where not infrequently I found a hamlet adjoining which men tilled small blocks of land, one below the other, that appeared to descend straight into the heart of earth. People lived in such hamlets frugally, content with their routine lives. The strong sun had browned their faces and shoulders, but their gaze reflected serenity of mind, having arrested life in its threadbare yet lovable form which the mountains had shielded for ages.

From time to time, I went to visit the librarian. Almost always he was to be found in the library, either sitting by the window listening to the stream that passed hundreds of feet below, or reading or tending to books. Occasionally, he agreed to take a walk through the garden of the abandoned church. Wild grass had all but covered the mud path that cut through the garden and ended at the edge of the precipice. There were lilacs and wild roses, and in patches where the grass had been unable to take root it was not difficult to pick out some old graves. The old man had an elfin step and I could keep pace with him only with slight effort. It reminded me of Achilles and the tortoise, a race where Achilles' quickness has no match for the slowness of the tortoise.

One day I found him in the rear of the building contemplating the mountains, a hazy pink at that hour, through a small window. A cool wind was blowing in short sudden gusts as if it descended straight from those lofty summits, evading the deep valleys and the trees and spirits that peopled them. His attendant had just served lemon tea, and he asked me to join. It was pleasant to sit there and wait for the night to fall in the hills. Then I asked him about the paradox. So, am I the tortoise? he chuckled.

We discussed the paradox – rather he spoke and I listened. One by one he took apart the refutations put forth by Mill, Bergson, and Russell. He quoted from memory several passages (even a few lines in Latin he didn't care to translate), and while he spoke, his voice grew excited and foreign by turn. Finally, he came back to Bergson, attempting to show the faults in his reasoning – something to do with divisibility of space and indivisibility of time or some such thing. From Bergson to Proust to Kazantzakis, the discussion went on for over two hours. By then the sky was a hazy violet and the evening star had appeared over the horizon. I said it was beginning to get dark, not realizing that his world had darkened already.

A hundred thoughts swirled in my head as I walked back to the cottage. In the growing dark, the silhouettes of trees appeared slightly diffused. I looked askance at them and increased my pace: a ghost could descend from one and trouble me with its lonesome tale. When the woods were behind me, I saw the stars enter the sky and make interesting designs. The dome of the club glowed softly. I thought of having a drink.

Days went on in much the same way. Time here was a pointless intrusion, and one would do all too well to stay clear of its awareness.

While writing one day an image grew on the page. Two forms wrestling on the floor, serpentwined, tearing and eating each other in a room luminous with heat. Now her warmth is entering me and so is the cold of the stone underneath and yet neither can fathom my depth. Later we are on the terrace. The sun is a useless orange disc over the horizon about to slide through the last chink in it. Nearby a kite flutters with wanton zeal. A tear has burst over my cheek. She is taking it on her tongue.

The image left me ill at ease. A longing had set in, a longing that grew with each moment, a longing that had traversed many a mountain and landscape, traversed the stretch of time, of life itself: a longing to touch her again. I had not thought of her in a while, but, for once, I felt she was close by. Perhaps this very moment she was wandering through the bazaar.

I walked out of the cottage into a slow wind. The sun had been anemic since morning, but now it was completely lost in the mist that clouded the sky and lingered over the mountaintops. From there it leisurely crawled down into the valley consuming all that obstructed its march. Soon I was climbing the hill that lay at the other end of the settlement. From there I could see but the last three cottages, for the mist had handsomely spread everywhere and chloroformed the pines.

Following a rough mountain track, I rounded that hill and the next. And after toiling for nearly an hour I came out into a clearing through which flowed a stream of crystalline water. It cascaded down the slope at the far end. At its bottom were very fine white pebbles. Tiny blue fish swam in it unaware of the happenings in another medium. They moved with a swiftness that excited the eye. The stream appeared to originate from under a huge rock covered in moss behind which swayed a few trees with purple flowers.

The mist had – almost incredibly – left the place untouched. Close by was a bamboo grove through which jutted wild yellow flowers. It was here that I entirely exorcised the phantom that plagued me. Into a corner I receded, resting my back against the tall, slender stems and looked above at the piece of sky left me. About me, birds and squirrels filled the air with their timeless melodies, and nearby the tiny blue fish sent tiny, soundless ripples to the surface of the stream.

X

It was one of those days that take birth prematurely, that once born neither breathe in the light nor in the dark, hanging aimlessly between the two. All day long, damp, solemn winds had been descending from the clouds – that had thrown the city into a perpetual twilight – and hinting at rain. The streets were quiet and gloomy, and not many people walked them. Traffic was sparse, its noise muffled by the moisture in the air. All in all, it was a day soaked in melancholy.

By this time I had spent two months in London. My only regular outdoor trips were to the neighbourhood library. At times I accompanied my sister to the supermarket, while at other times I went with her for a drink to her favourite club off Tottenham Court Road.

I had neither money nor debts, and was quite content to idle away my days reading and listening to music. That is when I began to think that there was something going on between books and music, jazz music to be specific.

A book is an enigma. Words that fill its pages present a shifty, relative universe. Through a reader, they create constructs where the past attempts to meet the future, the present arranging the meeting. In this present, as the reader receives and breaks apart the text – revives the past, contemplates the future – he, unknowingly, merges the two and makes the present fluid, expansive, eternal: he defeats time.

But the author waits for the reader in the heart of his labyrinth. Should one go in search of the other? And how? Here, at last, music comes to his help. Through its notes, variations and cadences, through its silences held tightly between its rhythm, the reader at last can glance into that inferno which is the centre of the maze, which is the long dead and yet still palpable soul of the author, for they are one and the same. Never believe the profane talk that goes around in certain places.

I had read Flaubert till late the night before, and awoke unmindful to the murkiness outside. In my sleep, I had had a dream where I happened to meet the Master. He was sitting in the garden of his stone house, contemplating the river as dusk fell over Rouen. I went strolling by, humming softly to myself. Then Flaubert called my name, and bade me to come inside. He looked handsome even in his corpulence and his eyes burned with creative passion. Offering me coffee, which tasted like the ink he must have used to write, he turned away once more to watch the river. Now in his solitude, it seemed, he often remembered Emma

Bovary. I had a suspicion that his days were like each other, filled with writing and masturbating, masturbating and writing. Life was one never-ending onanism between the bed and the desk. All of a sudden he looked at me. His eyes had turned on themselves, and his face resembled a sage in his moment of ecstasy. Had he been smoking something? I felt a distinct chill climb down my spine. I was shivering to tell the truth. Then, beneath the heavy moustache, his mouth twitched. Did I write? Somehow I took control of myself and said that I had felt the desire to write once or twice, but hadn't yet attempted it. Hearing this, he became excited: Don't let this streak die in you, my boy. It can help a writer in more ways than you may imagine. Look how I labour here, away from the joys of everyday life, away from love, to produce a work dear to me. Each day I wait for *this desire* to fill me, but alas it avoids me. I've to make up by endless hard work. By God, I find it hell to write. So the next time it strikes you, seize it with both hands.

The dream lingered in my thoughts while I prepared and ate a late breakfast, listening to Ellington and Coltrane by turn. I went over to the window. The clouds appeared so low and heavy that a finger would have punctured them. Soon someone had touched them, for a drizzle had erupted. I don't recall how long I'd stood there when I saw a girl walking in the street below, holding up a blue parasol to the heavens. She had a light step and swayed tenderly to some inner melody. I was overwhelmed by the image. Seize it with both hands, Flaubert's voice emerged over the strains of the saxophone. I hurried to the desk and, switching on the lamp, turned the cover of my red notebook. For a moment, the infinity of the blank sheet nauseated me. Then it came out thick and fast, like bodies in a bad crime novel. Once I couldn't go on anymore, I bent over my notebook and tried to touch the words fastened on the sheet. But they did not respond to my caress. All I felt was the smoothness of paper. My eyes grew moist. That night I slept well. A book had been born.

XI

Rest a moment dear storyteller, move with caution, else the thread may slip past your fingers and defile that which you have persevered to present with a restrained elegance. So take my advice and inhale deeply. Allow yourself for once to think of that night in Paris when the moonshine entered the two fastened bodies and cast its spell.

We reach the room in half unconsciousness. I totter about to the balcony. As I open the windows, the light filters in; on the wall behind her a Monet replica shimmers in its caress. A pleasant draught is blowing into the room. I know I must not let this moment pass. It will haunt me forever, I will feel its throbs far into time, it will break me bit by bit. But I let it pass, I touch that skin, I raise the hem.

Inside her is a desert and I slither like a snake in it. I look into her eyes; there is no life in them. She is staring through me straight into the void. A sudden panic makes me retreat. But she cuts it off halfway, tightening her legs around me. I am in her like a sword in its sheath. She moves and she takes me with her. I feel her hot breath on my brow and at last I fall into the sea.

When I awake, she is in the balcony, silhouetted against those facades, each a twin of the other. When she turns to look at me, the rays break into smithereens at her shoulder.

We went to Montparnasse to eat in a restaurant located in an alley off Boulevard Raspail. The sun did not reach into it and the shade emphasized the sky above. Somebody had hung out underwear to dry, and we had to duck quite low to cross to the other side. In times past the place had been frequented by not a few writers and artists. As was expected it was popular with both students and tourists, and attracted them in large numbers. Although full at that hour, we somehow managed to find a table near the counter. Behind it was a painting and a calendar. The painting was the work of some Cubist – a triangular face with both eyes on the same side, one below the other. The calendar was a few months behind. Waiters crisscrossed past the tables and the air was full of voices and the clatter of knives and forks. It was also full with the smell of buns and coffee.

Later we went to the library at Sorbonne. From its central courtyard, the dome glowed a bright purple in the noon sun. My task there was simple but exhausting: I wished to collect all of Sartre's love letters! And do what with them? I wasn't sure of that. Yet I busied myself with this absurd project. In two hours I had amassed nearly sixty. I was tired and further prospecting didn't excite me very much. I left it at that.

I join her. She has been reading from Proust. Outside in the street she tells me why she named me so: It's your eyes. The same round, slightly protuberant eyes.

That evening Amelio is playing at the jazz bar in St-Germain. He is on a trumpet, and a woman is lilting out words in a deep coppery voice. The song goes on for a while. After it is over, Amelio walks up to us and asks us to follow. With a glass of wine swinging between his fingers, he takes us up on the terrace. In a corner against the parapet, his knees fold and he sinks to the ground. Then he removes from his pocket a pack of cannabis that makes his eyes twinkle.

XII

How during those days the city spread its arms and how gladly we ran into them. We walked past those tombs in Père Lachaise. We lunched beneath the modern high-rises at the Grande Arche. We dined in Place Vendôme. We went to the Louvre. Under a chestnut in Bois we lay watching an airplane dash off the name 'L O L A' in the sky.

On one such evening, lost like a dream, we were walking up the Champs-Elysées when my sight fell on a beautiful silk scarf in a shop window. At once, I made a present of it to her and she wore it round her neck with something of an imperial air. We took the metro to Trocadéro and, walking through the complex, soon reached Pont d'Iéna from where you could see the ivory dome of Sacré-Coeur towering above the city at the far end. Below, the pier was brimming with activity as tourists embarked and disembarked the many ferries that took them along the river.

Bateaux Parisiens? I point to the boat. She nods her pretty head.

Then I had to go to Frankfurt to attend a writers' fair. It is important to be there, my publisher had told me. What could my books say to a reader in Germany, I thought, when they had said nothing elsewhere? I didn't have a good feeling from the start. The weather would only confirm this.

Heavy, bituminous clouds trailed low over Frankfurt and it rained almost all the time of my stay. When it didn't, a dense mist descended over the city. At night the sky over my hotel in Sachsenhausen was dark and luminous by turn. I longed to get back to Paris. And so I was only too glad when my plane landed there after two sombre days.

Finally I got to my place. Climbing up to my room, I began to wonder why the concierge had handed me the keys. Maybe she went out for a walk, I said to myself. The room had a stale air. The French windows were shut fast. I opened them and went out into the balcony. I stood there awhile watching the activity in the street. Slowly a suspicion had been taking hold of me, and its full blow turned me to stone for a moment. I ran into the room and leapt towards the cupboard. The tinkling of empty hangers resonated through my fast-hollowing heart.

The concierge was unable to help. He seemed even more baffled than me to be questioned like this. What else could I do, I set out to find her.

Once in the street, I knew not where to look. I began walking hurriedly but aimlessly. Spiders of anxiety were crawling down from the sky and weaving a frosty, oppressive web round me.

Amelio had told me in passing that he often played chess in the afternoon at a certain café on Rue de Lappe. I located it without much difficulty (instinctive faculties, it seems, were working with a miraculous lucidity). What relief the sight of him gave me! Sitting in one corner of the café, he was lost in an empty chessboard in front of him. Next to it, from a mahogany box, a black bishop was struggling to escape. A dense concoction of pain and anxiety had completely filled me up by then. I sank in the seat opposite, sweat collected on my temples and on the nape of my neck. My voice sounded not my own. He looked at me, but did not see my anguish. He was lost to some conundrum. I was beside myself, yet I asked him about it. It turned out that he had lost a game after months and was now pursuing the pieces in his mind's eye to their imminent doom. All along he kept caressing the bishop's crown that jutted out of the box. After this he rolled his eyes and broke into a soliloquy of sorts that, given my state, threw me into delirium: The game is a labyrinth. . .of unfathomable depths . . . It is a mirror of our lives . . . like chessmen, we move through days and nights. . .forever prisoners of glowing passions and dark reflections . . .

I didn't know how to interrupt him. When I got my chance, I said something. The words felt heavy against my tongue and seemed to burn holes in it. My mouth was dry, as if glazed with sand. At first, he absently stared at me, but then asked me where we had met before and if I'd not like a cup of coffee, for he was surely ordering one for himself.

By that time my head was throbbing madly and my face was flushed. A lone tear had burst on my cheek. The wind took it away leaving behind a prickling sensation. A sudden drowsiness overwhelmed me, forcing me to halt at a stall for a sip of water. From a billboard across the road, a model in a white blouse and a short skirt wearing a most distasteful shade of lipstick smiled at me.

I reached my room and, tired and depressed, sank into a deep sleep. I woke up late next morning. I hadn't eaten in a long time, yet felt only a slight hunger. I took a shower and had some soup at a restaurant. I retraced our movements of the previous days but she was nowhere. Slowly the anguish I had felt the day before changed into a mere heaviness of the heart.

A few days later I was walking up the Montparnasse cemetery when I saw an old man collecting dead leaves in a wheelbarrow. Watching him I could barely breathe. A terrible pain rose from the pit of my stomach. Tears of which I was unaware stretched over my eyes to form a film so dense that the world appeared nebulous, throwing me into a sort of white blindness.

At eight in the evening, the early September sun was a smudge in the sky and the Seine shimmered in its dying light. I had been sitting on a bench lost in the infinite ephemeral folds of water. The din of automobiles behind me did not trouble me. To my left, the Tower stretched its legs and watched over the city. I knew that Paris had nothing further to give me, that my stay was at an end.

XIII

Maybe all this never happened. Maybe it's part of a myth coming to me at birth. But why then have I held so close to my chest this slow roving sadness which knows not its own source and takes form unannounced, like clouds that build up in a clear sky from nowhere – this melancholy which has all but made me impervious to love or nostalgia?

I could write no more. Instead I took to walking each day for hours. In the woods that shone a deep green in the summer sun, I found new paths to the stream, and here I rested, dipping my legs in its plashing water. Emptiness gradually filled me and, for long periods, I'd gaze at my reflection in the water which the blue fish cut through with their sharp movements. They also cut through the dead skin of my soles, providing a free pedicure.

Finally two of my books had come. I thought of showing them to the old man. At our last meeting, he had gifted me a book by Carl Spitteler. *Olympian Springs*. An English translation from the time of the War. I decided to go the next day.

That night I had a curious dream. I saw myself running to the library, a miniature book in hand which was a torch too. It was intolerably heavy like a piece of a dying star, and soon my arm hurt from the burden. In its light I saw that I was moving on a giant chessboard. Above, the black arc was collecting blacker clouds. The wind had slowly turned into a gale, and the ghosts of trees performed a terrible dance in it. When I reached the clearing, the library had come apart from its base and was tilting over the abyss . . .

The swallow had flown in from the open window and was now perched on the desk. From there it watched me move, but soon jumped over to the window sill and flew off.

Late that morning, I went up to the library. The wind was heavy and it loudly whistled through the building's cavities. My shirt's collar fluttered madly in it. A light mist lingered on treetops and the sun glowed indifferently. But the building was there, solidly holding its ground. Inside, the old man was perched on a ladder, inspecting the spines in the topmost shelf of a cabinet. I shouted a hello. After this, what happened could have come from a movie, could have occurred in a dream. He started, lost his bearing, and came crashing to the ground. Shock numbed me. By the time I rushed to his side, he lay on the floor motionless, neck twisted to one side. A few drops of blood still trickled from his ear.

I was on the floor, transfixed, stupidly looking at him. The attendant came running from the kitchen. Then things happened very fast.

I remember being at the funeral that very evening. No elaborate rites were deemed necessary, for none knew of the man's religious inclinations. Three men had dug a small grave at one end of the garden next to the church. Roses and lilacs decorated the body wrapped in country linen. Those about me had the look of men merely concerned about performing their duty fittingly. I tossed my books into the grave.

I decided to leave soon. Grief was beginning to break the walls again. I busied myself in my work. It became an exhaustion, an obsession. I worked for hours on end, neglected my food, nearly ceased my walks.

When I hadn't spoken with anyone in over a week, I thought of going to the bar. The house-servant had returned to his village to attend a marriage in the family. Yet meals always appeared at the right time, though I never once saw another soul in the cottage.

The manager, too, was on leave and had gone down to the plains. I don't know why but I felt defeated. Two men were drinking beer in a corner, talking of past times and laughing aloud. I had a couple of drinks and went my way. For the next few days, I avoided the club.

A slow rising mist had come to drown the hills. The sun shone intermittently, vaguely, uninterestingly. The wind carried with it a chill which one wouldn't have called pleasant. I had progressed much during this time with the book, yet I didn't know how to end it. I decided to leave it in the drawer for some days.

Then one day I thought of the library, of the tombal silence that must now cover its walls. I was curious to learn what had become of it. Had it been abandoned like the church to the corrosive forces of time and seclusion? No, it was too early.

As I climbed up to the library, a faint orangey smell reached me. Just before the clearing, a tree had sprouted bright red flowers that made it look lavish. I approached the building from the side. Pigeons had built a nest in its cupola and they fluttered impatiently round it. But the place had a stillness as if it was even now in mourning. Then the silhouette of a woman came into view. Sitting on the steps of the library, her arms cradling her legs, her chin resting on her knees, she was observing the ruined façade of the church. A traveller, I thought, as I moved towards her.

XIV

Dreams and reality are but different chapters of the same book. Wasn't it Schopenhauer who said so? That book through which at times you drift serenely, while at other times you tramp with thoughts tied to your step like large, prehistoric stones closes one day. Then, as one chapter merges into the other, loses its distinctiveness, you begin to see the true, enduring wisdom of its words.

Astray I had wandered in these mists for long looking for a place to rest, to relieve my burden. But the mists did not depart. They collected around me and solidified like nebular dust. How much further? I cried despairingly. Whither do I belong?

I am barely a few steps away when the traveller turns towards me. Her face, tanned golden, is mysteriously elegant, smooth forehead, hair straight and lustrous that curls behind the ears. Her gaze pierces through me and I come to look into those clear brown eyes.

On her though, the effect is far serious. Her lips suddenly tighten and a stern look fills her face. A lone nerve is twitching on her forehead. She is about to weep. Now she is walking towards me. Uncontrollable tears roll down her cheeks. In a moment, she is in my arms, kissing and speaking at once. She is telling me it's been seven years.

So suddenly has all of it happened that I don't understand at first. Then a face grows over this one and I feel a stab in my heart. I pronounce the name slowly, with much difficulty.

She doesn't respond, but her hold tightens and her lips press against mine ever more intensely. I feel blood drain from my legs. At last I have seen dream and life coincide. I am closer to the end than I ever was. I am surer of it.

The weakness passes. We walk back to the steps and sit beside one another. For a seemingly long time none speaks. The mist pleasantly lingers around us. Pigeons beat their wings urgently, making a dry perfunctory sound. Her smell has evoked in me that one image, drawn in precise detail like a Flemish painting. From a valley far away rise up the bell-chimes of a village temple. The distant rhythmic chimes bring to mind another forlorn sound that has traversed the treacherous distance of memory.

Something has caught my attention. Her navel is decorated by the arabesque of a strange tattoo – a kite-like formation of inter-twined tails of numerous faceless serpents that from one end advances dangerously towards forbidden regions. Also, a fever is growing in her.

She begins to speak, but I say there will be time later. While we walk back to the cottage, her head is on my shoulder and our arms thread through each other. The wind rises and falls in the pines and only intermittently a word or a whole phrase reaches me. Stranded . . . Grey wastes . . . Pharaohs . . . A few words in Arabic . . . A name . . . Port of Alexandria . . . But I am far away from all of it, even from her. I have just seen the spot where I belong – have always belonged.

She refuses to eat, but she has taken a few sips from the cup I gave her. She says she wishes to lie down with me. Night is already entering the earth.

We are in the dark. She has fallen into a light sleep while I have been stroking her shoulders. Her breathing is heavy and comes in gasps. The warm air falls on my neck in lumps. But I am far away, on the sands that I will never see or touch. And later near the sea, near the vessel. She stands on the deck, and the moist cheerful air slips into her heart and drums its sundry rhythms on it. With one hand resting on the rails and the other at her hip how beautiful she looks.

Then she speaks slowly as if from inside a deep cave: Suppose I die?

Then I'll die too, I answer.

Why so?

Because one must share the fate of his loved one.

She has turned her back to me and I know she is looking out of the window. Her lean hips warm my groin. Past the branches of the deodar a yellow moon pours its shine into our hearts, a moon so low that the hills seem to cup it, overwhelmed all about by a thin darkness. Like a wolf or an owl the moon has bewitched me. An hour before dawn it turns golden and a procession of white clouds quietly passes over it.

At first glow I go over to my desk and pull out the pile of pages from the drawer. The house has grown hauntingly silent. Before I know the sun is high up in the sky and the swallow has alighted on the window sill to keep me company. Twice a light mist flows into the room. From time to time, the deodar becomes invisible. The world turns mute.

Light had left the hills when I went out. Outside the moon coloured the cottages a crimson white. The clubhouse with its blue dome looked like the retreat of a pasha. Soon I was descending into the valley. I crossed the bazaar where most shops had closed down for the day, while a few were tending to last-minute customers.

Before long I was walking (or drifting?) on a narrow mountain road that at some distance joined the main highway. It was pleasantly deserted. I must have walked a mile when my sight fell on a white chrysanthemum that lay at the edge of the road over a bed of wild mountain grass. It appeared unusually big and I was tempted to touch it. Now the moon was troubling me, glowing like the sun. I raised the chrysanthemum like a parasol and a cool shadow fell on my face.

All of a sudden, a slanting drizzle burst from the sky. I was drenched in no time, but the flower was completely dry. The rain had a curious effect on me – it roused forgotten thoughts and distant and enchanting sounds. In my mind's eye I saw Asya gazing pensively afar, while the clear water of the lake, the sky, and the mustard fields sang for her. This vision lasted only a moment. After this, I heard a motley collection of sounds, a few gaining prominence, one after the other, before falling back into silence. First came the cries of a baby from the cold desert of Mongolia. This was followed by a deafening laughter of a pod of whales from deep in the Pacific. Then rose up the bell chimes of a temple in the south. And finally I thought I detected the crisp, dry sound of two atoms colliding on a star seven worlds away. Yet all I heard were the melancholy notes of a lute.

The rain fell leisurely, lightly. In a few moments (for a few moments) I had jumped past time and space. Everything in the world, I whispered to the black vault, exists to end up not in a book like the Poet had believed but in man's heart.

But in my flight neither did I notice that I was walking in the middle of the road nor did I hear the rattling sound of the old tractor that had come dangerously close, its faint beam barely illuminating the road ahead. It hit me from behind with great force instantly breaking my spine. Blood filled my mouth, and I vomited it eagerly. The flower still in my hand, I nearly flew under the impact tracing a red arc on the ground, fell on the wet grass, and rapidly rolled down into the valley. My fall was interrupted by a pine with a split trunk where rest at last descended on the tired, broken body. Then a heavy darkness fell over me.

Having reached the end of the page, she quickly turns it over to read further. But there is nothing. A blank page glares at her. She halts for a moment, and then returns to the last page and reads it again, slowly, almost meditatively. When she looks away, dawn is breaking. Her eyes are moist with fatigue. She is tempted to close them. From the music player in a corner, rise up the strains of *Vivaldi's Cello Concerto in C Minor* drowning the stillness settling over her heart.

Two Travellers

He who is about to sing the fourth song is either a man or a stone or a tree.
Lautréamont

That is why he came here. For the silence that opens the door, that destroys this crumbling rampart hopelessly thrusting its lot in space – letting, for once, the watcher watch himself. Cold, of which he is unaware, is already closing him into the night. Mist lingers over the woods, and a half-burnt moon draws out streaks of light from the white ground. His sight is in the throes of leave-taking and he cannot be certain of the lone star that shines aeons away past the low drifting clouds, suddenly opening up to him the vastness of the universe. O you fiery, flaming orb! O you last frozen tear of the retreating deity! But never before has he felt his breath move with the earth. At last there is the rhythm he has sought in vain all along, in paint, in music, in words. At last he breathes for the wolf that prowls in the trees, for the lark that will sing on the morrow.

Hands which are nearly claws, stiffening and curling in, make him more and more into the fierce bird he loves, whose movements he has watched countless times for long spells, spell-bound – *those long pernings, the quivering poise, the wings lifted for*

the plummet drop, the wild reascent, fascinated by such extremes of
need, of pride, of patience, of solitude – his twin, if he can believe the
look of himself in the mirror or in the eyes of those he meets in
the street. Due to the contracture in the tendons of his fingers, he
holds the pen with difficulty. Not that much is left in him to work
with. In truth, he only writes a little for distraction, for in the
present state the piano is beyond him. And yet he can hear the
quiverings of a song, what he sees coming into being each day on
the page. A slow piece, with ever-widening silences, as in
Beethoven's Seventh, so that there is nothing but a bridge of
sounds suspended from dizzy heights, linking one upon another
deep oceans of calm. Or is it merely the sap behind language,
behind the words he has drilled big holes into, which has begun
to flow? Nothing to express, but a need to express.

More than ever, he now understands Bram's gouache, no
longer in the cottage, but securely fastened on a wall in his mind,
so long and hard has he stared at it: the wave rising from none
knows where into the heart, into the mind, leaving the hand
which moves the brush, flooding all the filthy logic, now
mingling, now divulging, here swishing through vast empty
spaces like a comet, there abstracted from time and serene like a
peak.

For most part of the day he lies in his cot curled in the usual
way, holding his knees tight to the chest, entering the darkness,
so he thinks, from whence he came, and drawing on the inside of
his eyelids a mosaic of faces and images. Towards the evening he
takes long walks in open cold, and upon returning to the cottage,
prepares a meal, rice and a vegetable stew mostly, and smokes
and drinks himself into oblivion. White Beaujolais at dinner, then
later his favourite whiskey and slim black cigars. He has no use
for his old car, which he will soon be giving away to the farmer's
son who helped him paint the two rooms last winter. At this time
of the year, the country roads are broken and slippery, and his
vision is too poor to permit the adventure of fast driving.

Days go by without meeting or speaking to anyone. Earlier he would not have been able to stand this quiet, now he lusts for it. Aside from checking up on his wife each day, he stays clear of the phone. It has beeped just once in the whole week; his publisher, the one other person who knows he is in Ussy, called to tell him that they were yet again planning to put up the accursed play in Berlin. Will he travel to Germany to direct it? He is sick up to his throat with the nonsense of those tramps to pass time and the debris it kicks up in papers with each rerun at a theatre. All this when he wrote it simply to travel into a memory of a painting seen in Germany before the war. That and the vaudevilles of his youth. And the waiting, yes, the waiting in unending queues to collect his ration from German soldiers. No, he replies, he is too old and too bored with it. What do they expect from him at seventy-eight? Last man left in the banquet.

Night falls quickly. For this he can only be glad. Mercifully, time slumbers in the depths, and he finds himself rocking back and forth in the cradle of his past: Look, look there, at the fir tree of his childhood which turned green a week before others in the yard. How he climbed up to its top and jumped without a thought, the low branches breaking his fall, and yet failing to think of the fall itself or his cracked skull against the cold hard earth. Same for the dive into the sea from Forty-Foot at Sandycove. Such perverse yearning for vertigo, such brave curiosity of the precipice.

He never did think far into the future; only the past ever held his interest. And maybe this is why he never thought too hard about leaving the easy certainty of a teaching post and running away to Germany, to the art galleries that would put air back in his lungs. Already it had become impossible for him to teach Ronsard and Racine to rich and thick students, hungry only for the crumbs he threw at them, nudging past one another to a bright academic career. How could he explain this to the professor who had arranged, in the first place, his move to Paris as a lector? And his father? He trembles at the very thought of that distant evening, of his father's pride on entering the private lawns of Trinity, which he had laid open with a key allowed only to the elect. The deepening hollow in his mother's eyes he has somewhat forgotten, but the bays and mountains of his youth are etched clear on his heart. And what of the time when the covert operation he worked in during the war was compromised by that infamous double-crosser who on the very night of betrayal had taken along his concubine to squander his reward in the brothels of Pigalle, the brown, nubile whores joining her and working him up in an orgy, unaware of his beautiful priest crucifix lying rolled up in a cheap underwear? Did he not once think of the spectacular horrors awaiting him on the other side of the night as he made his escape from Paris by the very skin of his teeth (the shivers came later, and so, inevitably, did the tears!), while the Führer's grey-uniformed phantoms got ready to make the arrest?

It seems to him that he has led all his life in a soft fog of memories. Whatever he has read and written, whatever he has heard and played, all that he has seen and done. Sounds and images come in flashes, while washing, cooking, walking, working. Everything he tastes, sees, touches, smells bursts into impressions. The solitary yelp of a dog reaching him from across the Marne is already that of many dogs barking in the stone quarries up in the hills in a night of his childhood. And now there is the figure of a black swan on an Australian stamp in his brother's collection. But before long the swan is vanishing in the sound of a cowbell tinkling in the pastures under the peak of Monte Generoso, which is reflected in the waters of Lake Lugano. And now there is the little boy urinating against the wall in the painting by Salomon van Ruysdael, and now the smell of his own piss rising from the hedge under a bottom-heavy moon over the village of Laxenburg near Vienna, and now the neat row of prostrate figures on a roof, their bottoms bronzing in the sun, and now the little patch of yellow in Vermeer's *View of Delft* that

Proust's Bergotte contemplates before killing himself, and now a wind-filled tree in a Cézanne landscape forever free from the gaze of man, and now the smoothness of a stone fished from the bed of the Rhine, and now the golden engravings on a pencil leaving a yellow shadow in the inside margin of a book's page, and now Joyce's inhuman lament at Lucia's worsening state and his own blindness, and now Valéry's explication how the *Wake* was nothing but a magnificent waste, and now the backbreaking work in the red farms of Roussillon, and now the agreeable weight on the spine of a sack of grain for chopping wood for the farm owner, and now the Irish sun slipping past the flowing mane of a galloping horse in the racetrack in Leopardstown, and now the stolen Staunton chess set of his father, and now that shiny black pawn about to be promoted on the board, and now Duchamp's voice telling of the invisible tears of rage and impotence welling up in him as he sat in the taxi clasping his *Nude* tight across his chest, and now the dirty chamber pot carried past a group of people at lunch in the middle of the day, and now the joy of mounting a camel in the Sahara, and now the inverted moon seen in the curve of the Atlas Mountains, and now the silhouette of a woman waiting in a Tangier teahouse, and now a line of Dante, and now the clear image behind that line, and now an old, wrinkled face in a frosty night, and now the beat of his own steps, and now the delicious sound of the club hitting the ball on the golf course in Belfast, and now that moment of pure emptiness that makes the sound delicious, and now the fall back into the mess of existence, and now the lilt of a trumpet in a jazz bar in Holland, and now the red in the Mandala on the wall of that bar, and now the taste of blood in his mouth, and now those resigned yet definitive words: *Je ne sais pas, Monsieur. Je m'excuse,* what charming manners!, and now the words merging to form that one word he has been trying to make for years, a word as long and hard as an excited member, and now the swing of the heavy blade chopping the member free of the body, and now the sound of his wife working on the sewing machine in her room, and now the look in her eyes that bespoke not just despair and anger at his nights of dissipation, but pity, both for herself and him, and that other thing which he can't put into words but only compare, to what?, yes, that look he saw in the eyes of Artaud sitting lost in a café in Saint-Germain-des-Prés so many years ago, a look that will die with him, for he knows he was its sole witness.

Not another time, he had told himself, will he wander. Not again could he hold inside him that look in her eyes. But love by then had already left his bones, like a tide on ebb, and was held back only by a weak flesh. Thus the promise was forgotten one evening in Berlin, though this was not intended.

Rehearsals had not been going well. The ashcans, in spite of everything, were not exactly as he had seen them in his head. The actors were simply overdoing it. Too much colour, he kept repeating, too much colour. He had walked back from the Academy, unable to enjoy the view of the river. Is it ever possible to be true to an image, he wondered? Swiftly cutting through the trees, he entered the café opposite his studio, which went by the unlikely name of "Giraffe." The fare was ordinary, to say nothing of the wine, but the place was quiet on most evenings and made him feel at ease. And before he knew, the woman he had agreed to meet there was speaking to him. First he answered without looking, smoking away absently. But presently he turned, and it was the angle that did him in. The yearning sprang at him with a simple twist of the neck. The first and last thing he saw was the milk-white earlobe with a beautiful pearl in it, entirely free of the dark hair that soared and coiled up right behind the head into a soft ball. His legs began to shake and, for a moment, like in Proust, he went deaf. This dreary world, it occurred to him, was also the best of all worlds. Like a hologram, it gleamed with a mere tilt of the arm.

He wakes up in a sweat. Even after hours he is not free of the dream. In his own garage, he saw a large iguana in birth pangs behind a red sports car, watched, at the same time as himself, in terror and fascination by a man he surely knows well but about whom he seems to have forgotten everything else.

Outside a thrush is singing in the cedar grove. He leaves his oak desk and, taking the water flask off the shelf, drinks from it greedily. Looking at these trees he planted years ago and which he has carefully tended through so many harsh winters fills him with a sudden longing for this earth which, he is well aware, he should soon be leaving. Two months, two years, not much more. The trunk of that blue cedar, he tells himself, already carries all the wisdom of Goethe and Shakespeare. A pity it has taken him so long to see the simple fact. The eye deceives. The eye cannot truly see until the last tear has been expunged. Which, of course, isn't the case with him.

Yesterday he found a flute in the cottage. His nephew's surely. Distractedly, he blows into it and from its modest wooden depths rises, note by note, a strange, tremulous melody as if heard from the ends of the earth or such as coming to him uninterrupted from a night of some ancient race beneath ancient star clouds. The bird watches him, ready to respond. But instead of the birdsong he hears a faint, unmistakably Irish voice reciting, no, singing with a slow soft breath the words of his youth, penned one damp, drunk and homesick afternoon in a bar in Soho. *Oh hand in hand let us return to the dear land of our birth, the bays, the bogs, the moors, the glens, the lakes, the rivers, the streams, the brooks, the mists, the–fens . . .*

Try as he might, he cannot put a face to that moving voice, he who has seen so many faces in dreams and waking. Burying his chin for warmth into the loose collar of his much-worn ash-blue turtleneck, he moves his tongue over the growth in his mouth which doesn't pain him anymore. His mind is elsewhere, igniting the fire of memory by fanning the embers. Suddenly the flames are glowing and leaping higher and higher, and a smile slices his

lips after many days even as he wipes away the tear that is about
to drip.

*

The boat is bobbing up and down on the waves. Beneath an
indigo vault heavy with stars, so many that they make a complete
mess of the designs the ancients saw in them, the air is neither
cold nor warm. He has removed the oars from the water and is
rubbing his palms to calm the blood coursing through them. In
the distance he can see the lights twinkling on the shore, and
beyond these he can feel the mountains rearing their dark bulk.
Across from him, his blind companion, his arms clasping the
plank on either side, is alertly listening to the plash of water on
the timber as if he can detect in it the rumble of clouds over an
unknown planet.

At last I could write no more, breaks out his companion, on
this, their third night together. At thirty-eight, I had tired of aping
Quevedo or Thomas Browne. My bag had become empty of
tricks. During this time, my father, who had been for a while
impatiently waiting for death, died. I was heartbroken. He had
taught me so much, given names to all my curiosities of
childhood. Soon thereafter took place the accident I spoke of last
night at dinner, recovering from which, almost in a spirit of
learning to think again, I wrote my first real story.

He has been quietly listening. Yet somewhere inside him is the
other who is recalling his own thirty-eighth year. Heartbroken.
The very word he would have chosen. His beloved father long
since turned to mud in the yard of that sorry old family church.
And then the night when, watching over his unwell mother and
reading Stevenson's *Letters*, a window had suddenly opened on
the mouldy cell where he had been slowly suffocating. Throw
away everything you have accumulated over the years. Rid
yourself of all the tricks, and get down to finding the funda-

96

mental . . .

A few months before, carried on the other, I had taken up the first regular job of my life, predictably enough, at a municipal library, out in a dull southwest corner of the city. There were too many of us doing the simple work, classifying and cataloguing the library's holdings. Naturally, my colleagues were more interested in betting on horses, telling obscene jokes and stories, and listening to soccer matches on the radio. Each day I catalogued about hundred or so books. Even with my failing eyesight, I could have easily classified four or five times that number, but I had been forewarned against being too enthusiastic in my work which could reflect unfairly on others. So having finished the task by noon, I'd repair to the basement of the building where, in a staff reading room, I read till it was time to go home. It was here that I read all of Gibbon, Bloy, and Bernard Shaw. It was here that I did those translations of Faulkner and Woolf which enjoyed some measure of success in my country. And it was here, in this modest, forgettable building wherein, ironically – but, well, there is no irony in it – I wrote of that infinite, monstrous Library which marred my dreams each night, picking up facts at random from the very room I sat in, and mixing them with anything I happened to be reading just then. Those ciphers, he says teasingly, have been endowed with undue mystical importance by readers who know nothing about this period of my life.

He is enjoying it. Listening to this soft, slow voice, moving carefully in the dark like a panther, the Irish tinge in it now and then rising above the sound of the lake. He lights up one of his slim cigars and blows on it leisurely. His companion can smell the tobacco on the air and breathing in once or twice continues.

Sometimes in the evening when I took the tram to return home, my eyes would fill up with tears. Mostly I'd be reading Dante. Although I remembered a fair bit by heart, I'd keep on reading, and soon the book would begin to lose its letters and grow more and more empty, until finally I was staring into a creamy eternity whereon the tears were freely falling. And then I'd remember Epictetus. Remember that the door is always open. So if I couldn't muster the courage to end it all in one stroke, I'd do better to wipe away the tears. Next day, however, it would start afresh. Such is the sameness of our lives. Such is human feebleness. Why bother moving when you can only arrive at that from which you left? On and on I went like this for a good nine years. I know not why though. Maybe because I had gotten used to the drab routine of my days. Maybe because I was carried away on the thrust of the work I was then doing; work, which people today generously call my best. Or simply because time had already begun to set me free for my approaching blindness.

Speaking now for the first time since he rowed them out here, he tells of his school copy of Dante with his notes scribbled in the margins from fifty years ago to which he returns whenever he reaches a stasis in his work. Superstitiously, perhaps, he feels he will find there something new to begin. After all, he says in a voice barely perceptible, it was with Dante that it all began. The motion in stasis, and stasis in motion. The moving unmover.

The Comedy, says his companion eagerly, is, of course, the greatest work in all the literatures of the world. In its cosmology, I don't believe for a minute, and yet it is the book I love the most. As for the moving unmover, one may look also at Zeno or the sophist, Gorgias of Lentini, who could well have been behind Kafka.

He nods from the opposite side of the boat, but this his companion cannot see who is silently reproaching himself for interrupting the other with his silly enthusiasm.

For a while none has spoken. Only the sound of water crashing against the boat fills up the silence, which is also another form of silence. He is thinking about the discussion they had earlier in the day, first regarding chess, the domain of the inexplicable for it has in it the light and the dark together, and later, Joyce and *Finnegans Wake*. His companion, an early champion of Joyce in the South, didn't have much admiration to spare for the *Wake*. He wonders now whether he himself believes what he had said then: the *Wake* being the only possible development from *Ulysses*. That if the latter was the utterance of thought observing itself, the former was the very speech of the dreaming mind. As they row back to the shore, the lake sighs with each move of the scull.

How do you put in words the sound of water beating the wood? asks his companion. Better still, says he, how do you enter it? Earlier, arm in arm, we went to the cove from where you learnt to dive as a child. Did you hear the terrible cries of the gulls in the lee of the rampart? How easily they crawled into the roar of the tides, carried away who knows to what eternity. . .

He does not respond. The last few days have taught him at least this much: his companion is extremely shy and so almost all his questions are rhetorical. And, sure enough, before long the other is speaking.

My sight was always poor. I could see faces clearly only in photographs, by bringing them under my nose, by breathing over them. Thus I saw not the Viking swords in Yorkminster, but the hot Saxon blood they spilt on the ground centuries ago. Thus Buenos Aires is not a city but a habit for me. That is why many who have come to it through my writing have found it empty except place names, anecdotes, and a few friends. The markers of the blind. But I deviate. To return to the sound, to the water. . .

All through the War, my family stayed in Geneva and, oblivious to the happenings beyond the borders, I joyously swam in all the rivers of the Swiss country. Like a fish I went along and the flow of water which is also its sound entered my flesh and bones, writing its script in them. The same script I later divined in the spots of a leopard.

All these many years, it seems to me, I have just wanted to enter this sound. I can hear it in the words I keep rolling in my head. Yet what do I leave behind? Stillborn ideas. Empty scratchings on paper. Words, words, words. That prison from which I have been unable to rid myself. Exiled in myself, like Hamlet. It is in such moments that I completely grasp the agony of Shakespeare, lord and slave of words. It is in such moments that I become Shakespeare.

There came a time when I was an exile in my own country, amid banners and slogans, amid – what after a fashion was called – the deafening march of history into the future. Exiled in my body, exiled in words, and finally exiled on land as well. A land to which my ancestors gave their blood. A land whose vast wind-rowed wastes alone were enough to wet my eyes. A land whose glories I never did cease to sing, whether through its poets or its hoodlums. And then nearly in a whisper, a land I love almost physically, perhaps this is what I am often accused of – why only physically?

In America, says his companion, in Boston, a city I love, and I love many cities, I saw, no, only heard, but also felt deeply, your play of the man listening to his voice on tape. . .and the moment on the punt with the girl stretched out on the floorboards, hands crossed under her head, eyes squinting in the sun, and underneath all moving, all astir. . . A symphony of sounds taking you past knowledge into knowing. An image granted not through words, but in spite of them. A real image, not a label on the image. Expression in art, which Croce demanded from the artist, is mere vanity, a great mistake, as you have shown in your work. My gods, on the other hand, grant me only allusion.

On a sudden inspiration, his companion begins to recite in German a poem of Heine. He has not seen before eyes light up so at the sound of words. These are not the eyes of a blind man, eyes with a child's innocence in them. So moved is he that he too joins in, at first under his breath, then boldly mixing his voice with the other:

. . . Als ich nach Hause ritt, da liefen
Die Bäume vorbei in der Mondenhelle,
Wie Geister. Wehmütige Stimmen riefen –
Doch ich und die Toten, wir ritten schnelle.

They have reached ashore, and he has moored the boat alongside the jetty. Now he helps his companion on to the pier and hands him his stick. In truth, only last year he was himself half blind, but the surgery on his cataracts has, for the time being, restored his vision. They walk away from the lake, the one on the arm of the other, matching their steps to the measured beat of the stick on the ground. He has always found something utterly compulsive in the sound of steps. He can hear not only their own, but hundreds and thousands of tired steps crisscrossing this tired, deformed earth of his. Unending line of steps, of men, women, and children, poor and hungry and homeless, armies of battle-fatigued warriors, prisoners of so many gulags and camps with lost, weather-beaten faces, young whores running away from their tormentors, inconsolable souls wasting away from their love of metaphysics, animals collapsing under strain of their load, little steps, giant steps, steps, steps, steps, walking from one horizon to the other, from there to another and another and another, and then only the pendular movement of the prisoner in the Santé Prison he has seen so many times from his apartment window, and then it is not the prisoner he sees, but the beast in the cage, taking the world with him, from sense to nonsense, from nonsense to sense, with its every turn, this beloved tiger of Señor Borges.

Thank you, says Señor Borges pressing his elbow a little more firmly, for the boat ride, for bringing me here, for everything you have said and done, for all that you have taught me these past few days. How many times since we left Paris have I told you of my love for this place, dearer to me than even the red maze of London.

He shakes his head silently, and in turn threads his own arm through the other's, overwhelmed by emotion, unable to respond. No more is necessary, for the hint has been understood.

Let us now go and eat and drink, resumes his companion. There I will bore you with an idea of a story I just this minute discovered, about a rose that is made immortal by the name 'rose', and in return you may tell me how the moon is tonight. That we are here, without anyone knowing it, is nothing short of a miracle, which I produced simply by walking up the street and pressing the bell to your apartment, while all around us they break their heads and spines over our work, suffocating it under oceans of words and mountains of paper.

Academic dementia, he breathes in the ear of his companion, tightening his hold on the other's arm, and the two men break into laughter and song together, *the bays, the bogs, the moors, the glens, the lakes, the rivers, the streams, the brooks, the mists, the—fens . . .*

*

He lies sprawled on the wet grass thinking of Macedonio, a cold compress on his head, slowly forgetting the world, himself, and his quest, divining the truth in the middle of the pampa. What does he care that to his left at some distance, clouds are biting away and spitting ice on Mont Blanc? What does he care that he is back in the beloved city of his youth where he first found Schopenhauer and Whitman? For he can now see the tiger clearer than ever before, flying through the heat-shimmering jungles of Bengal, gathering speed, salivating, as it rushes to tear him to pieces.

A Word on Two Travellers

Fiction, once remarked André Gide, was history which could have happened. The evidence that Jorge Luis Borges and Samuel Beckett met in real life is scant and unreliable. This conclusion is supported by their respective conversations, interviews, and correspondences published to date, where one is conspicuous by his absence in the other. And yet their international renown owes so much to the First *Prix Formentor* the two writers shared in 1961. The prize opened up for their works new commercial possibilities, led to translations into several languages, and won for them innumerable admirers around the world. Proceeding with the assumption that the singular event of a meeting between the two writers never transpired is in some way liberating for a storyteller, for it grants him the occasion to weave fantasies into the texture of that which we call real.

Growing up in completely different and yet not so different worlds of Buenos Aires and Dublin in the early part of the last century, both Borges and Beckett were exceptional readers and dreamers from early age. Borges loved English as much if not more than Spanish and once remarked that English should have been his by birth right. Fueled by his father's love and passion for English writers and philosophers, he had by the age of nine already translated Oscar Wilde's *Happy Prince* into Spanish, which the publisher unknowingly but not unreasonably ascribed to the father instead of the son. Troubled by poor vision from the beginning, his father's library became for Borges the entire world, and it seemed to him later that he never did step out of it. Books, yes, but two other 'heterogeneous' (the word is a favourite of Borges or at least his translators) interests would divide and occupy him, remaining lifelong obsessions: chess and the tiger.

It is told that the child, taken to visit the zoo once, went up close to the cage due to his near-sightedness (hence, he once retorted that he preferred reading Milton in a hotel room in Paris to touring the city, and that he didn't ever regret it) and watched with wonder the toing and froing yellow-striped beast, which would mark thenceforth nearly all his hours of dream and waking, and which he would make eternal through his work, like Keats's nightingale. As he grew older, Borges would chase that one image through the works not only of Kipling and Blake, Dante and Whitman, but also through the writings of the Gnostics and the Chinese Mystics, giving to the tiger's stripes the 'secret language of God,' and ultimately employing it as a metaphor for that 'greatest of perplexities' – time – in the now famous words 'time is the tiger that destroys me, but I am that tiger.'

Then again, the chequered board became, like the wild cat, something mysterious, inexplicable, and necessary. Borges tells of his father using a chessboard to explain to him in his childhood why the arrow in Zeno can never leave the bow and how the nimble-footed Achilles will always lose the race to the crawling tortoise. As he grew to love Homer and Dante, Shakespeare and Cervantes, his love of the epic and beauty in literature coalesced with the enigmas of numbers and time into the black-and-white board, and gradually chess began to percolate into his stories, essays, and poems as an essential metaphor for that which is at once beautiful and elusive.

A few years spent in Europe, chiefly Switzerland, Spain, and Germany, from when he was only fifteen, exposed the young Borges to the flavour of other tongues and literatures, and which flamed his precocious talent for words, languages, and etymologies, acquiring and assimilating them with an uncommon delight. Thus, by the time he was all but twenty he had taught himself to read Heine in German, Dante in Italian, Baudelaire in French, and Virgil in Latin. At the same time his love for the English language and the literatures of England, Ireland, and America, reached a high point. He travelled widely in Spain and Germany where he perfected his strokes in fast-flowing rivers, fell under the spell of German Expressionist Art, met artists and poets and, uncharacteristically, even joined a literary group (which he later dismissed as a hoax) before returning to South America where he remained for nearly all his life, and composed the works on which his reputation most solidly rests. In his fifties, he succeeded the blind French historian, Paul Groussac, as the Director of the National Library of Argentina, by which time he was himself blind, a fact he attributed in a poem to the terrible irony of God who had given him 'books and the night.'

Beckett, on the other hand, grew up equally at home among books, music, and the outdoors. Sports came naturally to him and from a young age, he played cricket, tennis, and later golf, exceedingly well. While still a child, he accompanied his father on long walks into the Irish country and learned to dive and swim in the sea. The elemental in nature and the sounds and scenes of his childhood would have a lasting impression on him and remain a lifelong obsession entering and transforming his work everywhere. He received music lessons at a relatively young age and played the piano almost professionally as he grew older. Like Borges, he seems to have had a great talent for languages and by the time he had passed school he could already read books in French and Italian without help of a dictionary. In due course, he would teach himself to read German and Spanish too, becoming proficient enough at least in German to later oversee the translation into the language of some of his own work, and to travel to Germany to direct his own plays. Then again, like Borges, he succumbed early to the lure of the chess-board, not only becoming in later years proficient enough to play and hold his own against the likes of Marcel Duchamp, but to make it the very genesis of more than one of his important works. At Trinity College Dublin, he excelled in both sports and literature, often touring with the college teams for rugby and cricket tournaments and yet receiving a scholarship to become a lector in English at the École Normale Supérieure in Paris for two years.

Once in Paris, he quickly came into his own. Having been introduced to James Joyce, Beckett soon became a member of Joyce's inner circle which included leading writers and artists of the time. Much taken in by the senior writer, he often read and scribbled notes for Joyce's *Work in Progress* as his sight declined severely over the next few years, and later accompanying him for evening walks along the Seine. Encouraged by Joyce, Beckett collaborated with a friend to produce the first translation into French of *Anna Livia Plurabelle*.

By the time he came to Paris, Beckett already possessed a thorough knowledge of French literature and drama, and had carefully read the philosophical writings of Descartes, Geulincx, and Malebranche. During his stay there, he reread Dante's *Comedy* and began a systematic study of Marcel Proust's novel. Over the next decade, he would work with the Surrealist camp in Paris, contribute important essays on Joyce and Proust, publish his early poems and stories in avant-garde magazines, and translate into one another from French or English several crucial works. Following the natural course from Kant to Hegel, he one day came to Schopenhauer in whom he found 'an intellectual justification of unhappiness,' a support for his deepening view that suffering is inseparable from human life, that 'will' is an unwelcome intrusion, and that real consciousness lies beyond human cognition. Together with his previous readings of the Bible, the Greeks, and the Hermetic texts, he had acquired at least a working knowledge of Eastern philosophical systems. Newer discoveries in physics and mathematics drove him to the under-standing that reason beyond a point breeds paradoxes for itself, and that it is impossible to know reality through language, a view then becoming popular through the writings of Fritz Mauthner and Ludwig Wittgenstein. Side by side, he consolidated his knowledge and love of European Art, from old masters to the new, travelling from one gallery to another, in England, France, Italy, and Germany, even as the clouds of fascism were gathering ominously over Europe. Pilgrimages taken in tough times, with little money and through bitter cold, amid ever-growing swamps of destitution and desperation, and in a body already giving signs of suppuration would confirm his view that the 'experience of modern man is of a non-knower' and would push him away from those certainties of language and order, that desire of 'defrocking the object' to which Joyce and Proust had given their lives – push him to beget his grandest works in what he often called 'the great siege in the room.'

Since words alone were insufficient, Beckett took help from music and painting. Whether riding a bicycle, or leaning on crutches, or worst come worst, slithering on the ground like Molloy to find his mother (what in a Jungian analysis would be a move towards the *anima*, to the feminine in man's psyche in touch with the unconscious), Beckett continued to move on and on from one text to the next in his search for the 'real' which is at once revealed and curtailed by words. To pierce the curtain was to risk losing the 'real' itself, and so he did what was only reasonable: to employ words, like music and painting, in an abstract and essentially different, non-representational sense, to fish out, what Northrop Frye called, 'a truth of implication, a truth emerging from inner coherence rather than external reference.' What he had written before the war in his essay on Joyce's *Finnegans Wake*, became the first premise of his own writing '. . . form is content, content is form . . .'

The everyday reality which Beckett questioned in his work, had been from the very beginning suspect for Borges due to his poor vision, and which obliged him to see things a little differently from others. In addition to this, nearly all his earliest readings, from Mark Twain to Poe, from Grimm's *Fairy Tales* to Carroll's *Alice Books*, from *Treasure Island* to H. G. Wells to the

Arabian Nights opened up for him a different and richer world. With the passage of years, he read countless books, many that none had read for centuries, saw and heard terrible things, and divined that each seemingly ordinary day is also the carrier of untold silent cruelties, that which others give the name of 'reality' is a mere Schopenhauerian objectivation of will and thus in itself a fiction, far apart from the 'real' which is 'obedient to vast and secret laws' and, by its very nature, unknowable. But if the life we led, he asked himself, was essentially a fiction, could he not then bend it around his own designs to create, like Tlön, a minutely detailed orderly planet, 'a labyrinth forged by men, a labyrinth destined to be deciphered by men.' And yet to do so, it was essential to write in a fashion that would declare its own artifice, behind which there was nothing but an ever-widening black hole – that words were what remained to conceal the terror of the universe. But he took his task only ironically and never vainly so that later he could give, in one of his parables, the following epiphany to Giambattista Marino who understood on his deathbed that 'the tall, haughty volumes that made a golden dimness in the corner of his room were not (as his vanity had dreamt them) a mirror of the world, but just another thing added to the world's contents.' As Paul de Man observed early, 'his main characters are prototypes for the writer, and his worlds, are prototypes for a highly stylized kind of poetry or fiction . . . [constituting] Borges's distinctive style, as well as his comment upon this style. His stories are about the style in which they are written.' So, just as Beckett, form became content, and content form.

If one looks past their seemingly different works and styles, Borges and Beckett share an affinity in philosophy and vision that is uncannily close. Physically separated by vast spaces, their imaginary worlds as also their likes and dislikes in literature and elsewhere superimposed and dissolved into each other: from the love of Dr Johnson and Robert Burton, Joyce and Stevenson,

Heine and Schopenhauer, to the regard for Kandinsky's oils and Stravinsky's scores; from the sublime, abstract pleasures of chess and mathematics, the cosmologies of Milton and Dante, to the distaste for the philosophies of Heidegger and Sartre. What Beckett admired in Proust, Borges had long since found in the opium-induced dreams of De Quincey. That which had moved Beckett to write in his *Proust*: 'habit is the ballast that chains the dog to its vomit,' made Borges repair to the library and, circling in its dim sanctuary, produce a literature of order and splendour, unbelievable yet essential. And did not Beckett truly come to stand in for Borges – the dreamer who believed he had dreamt the world and forgotten about it – in *Comment c'est*, when he wrote, '. . .*but all this business of voices yes quaqua yes of other worlds yes of someone in another world yes whose kind of dream I am yes said to be yes that he dreams all the time yes tells all the time yes his only dream yes his only story yes. . .*'?

But what these two great writers shared above all, what one rarely finds in literature these days, was man's foredoomed quest to know his place in this gouache of space and time that he can't rid himself of, that which is both his prison and the window out of the prison, that which makes for both love and defeat, that which, for want of something better, he calls the universe.

Acknowledgements

Some of the stories collected in this volume first appeared in *Variaciones Borges, Arts & Opinion, Evergreen Review, Southerly,* and *Carpe Articulum Literary Review.*

The words in italics on pp. 89-90 and 95 are from Samuel Beckett's *Malone Dies,* p. 185 (The Grove Centenary Edition, Volume II: Novels. 2006. Grove Press, New York), and *Murphy,* p. 272 (1957. Grove Press, New York), respectively. The Heine fragment in German on p.101 is from the poem 'Wiedersehen' and can be found, among other places, in the bilingual collection, Heinrich Heine, *The Lazarus Poems.* Trans. Alistair Elliot (1979. MidNAG–Carcanet, Manchester).

At Roundfire we publish great stories. We lean towards the spiritual and thought-provoking. But whether it's literary or popular, a gentle tale or a pulsating thriller, the connecting theme in all Roundfire fiction titles is that once you pick them up you won't want to put them down.